Babington's Treasure Map

The code of the map was not deciphered for over one hundred years and then it became one family's mission.

By

David Kentish

Disclaimer

Although this story takes advantage of certain events which are recorded in history, none of the characters are based on any person either living or departed.

With the exception of the MacKay family who settled on Mundabullangana Station in the Pilbara District of Western Australia in the 1800's. They have a grand history of their own which is well documented by others.

Many sailing vessels have names which have been handed down through the centuries and although some may have been used in this story or may seem similar to others, there is no intention of the author to harm or defame any organisation, person or family.

David Kentish

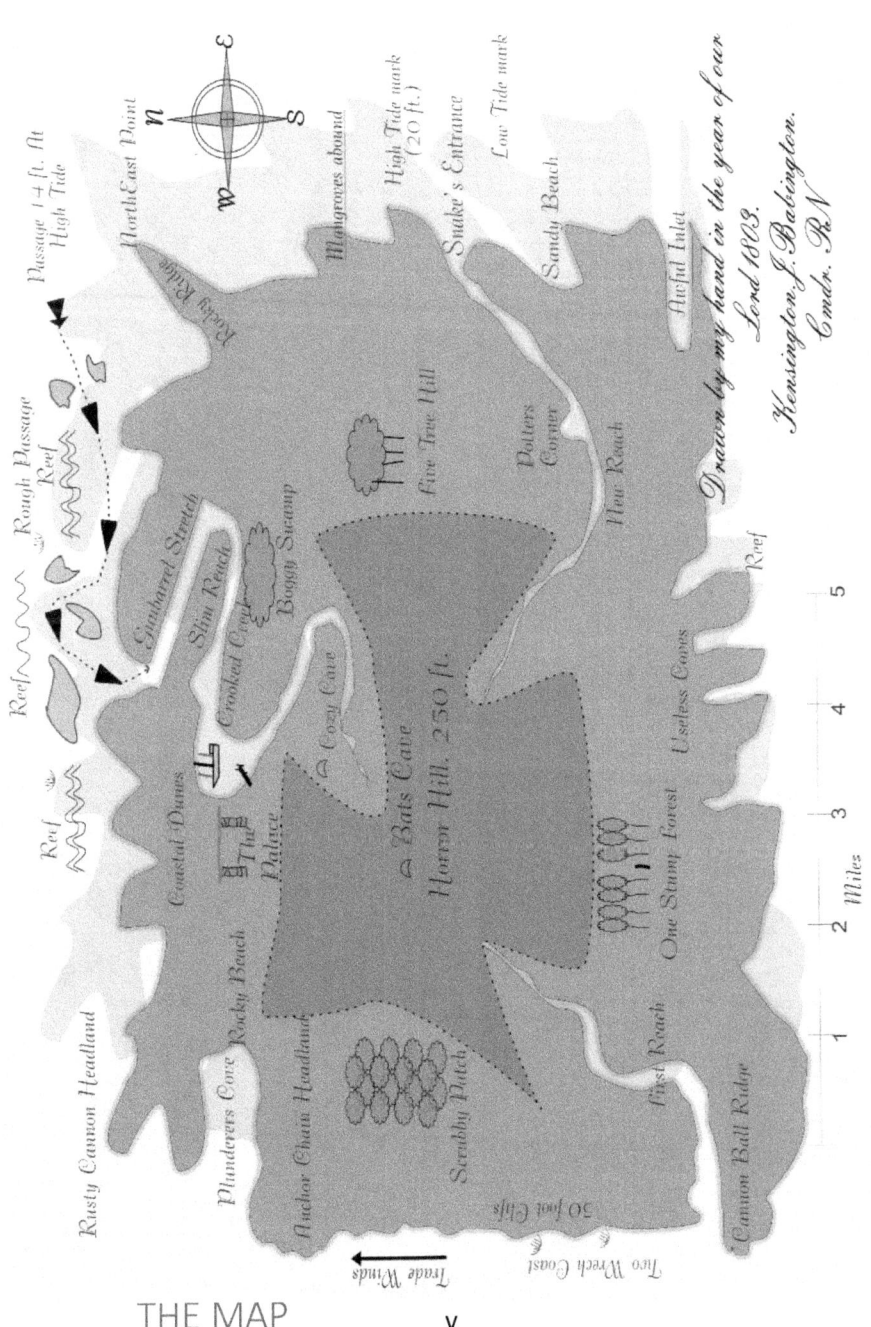

THE MAP

Contents

Chapter One

The three masted square-rigged ship was built in 1787 and named after the planet closest to the sun, Mercury. The Merkurius was Dutch built for the Vereenigde Oostindische Compagnie (Dutch East India Company) or the VOC as it was so called in its day. The shipbuilders took great care to meet the specifications of the VOC with the extended hold and extra sail area.

Instead of the usual two inch thick below the waterline timbers, these were of three inches thick to allow for a more robust hull and increase the cargo load. Above the waterline the hull timbers were back to the regular two inches of thickness. While still providing excellent robustness, it reduced the weight of the hull. The main deck and the upper deck were planked with oak, while the others used a lighter pine.

The upper and main decks are where the new cannons and extra ammunition are located and because of their extra weight, this provided a much greater strength than the lighter pine.

The deck cannons were of the latest design with the largest of these being cast from the new bronze/iron alloy which made them not only more robust but also, they could be loaded with a greater load of gunpowder and a heavier shot. This made this vessel one of the most modern and feared fighting ships on the ocean but also able to carry a large cargo.

All the sails were newly made from flaxen canvas and the ropes from newly spun hemp. Some of the halyards were as thick as a man's forearm.

The ship's crew were a seasoned lot as the company wanted to send out the best for their last few years as a trading company with the base at Batavia in Java. As the crew had been on other VOC ships, they were well trained. On the several voyages which had already been completed, they had drilled and had become a highly efficient team, each backing the other in case of need. Not only did they prepare, load, aim and fire the large deck guns, but there was also the hand-to-hand combat which they would be required to participate in from time to time. And they became very efficient at this task.

Usually, this ship while lightly loaded and under full sail in a ten-knot breeze would travel along at about eight knots, so they had one of the fastest and most efficient ships on the seven seas.

The skipper of the Mercurius is Captain Claus Herman DeJong. he has been the skipper of this ship for the last seven years and has completed three return trips from Batavia back to Enkhuizen in Holland. He has taken exceptional care to make sure that his crew was one of the best trained crews within the VOC.

This was to be his last trip, as upon his return to Enkhuizen, he was to retire to his small holding and grow tulips with his wife. She already was producing some very fine blooms and he was eager to join her and assist with production of more of these world-famous blooms.

After leaving their home port of Enkhuizen in Holland it takes about three months to travel to Batavia. Because of the issues that they have with the British, they do not travel down the English Channel but head West from their home port until they clear the north islands of Scotland and then head Southwards down the Atlantic Ocean. They crossed the equator after about three weeks, where the crew always holds a short ceremony.

While keeping close to and just insight of the West Coast of Africa, they round the Cape and visit Cape Town to top up their food supply and fresh water before they head further east and use the Tradewinds to their advantage to get back to Java.

The trade winds carried them to the Southwest Coast of Java, and they enter the Sunda Strait and then head east to the port of Batavia.

After four weeks in the port of Batavia, they had replenished their supplies on the ship and loaded the cargo which is necessary for the return trip back to their hometown. With this being the last ship to leave the port of Batavia, there is also several office workers and their families who board for the return trip home.

From the port of Batavia on the northwest Java coast, it was almost fully laden when it departed the wharf area, homeward bound, via the port city of Surabaya to the east. The tide was high and because of the gentle breeze, the going was slow.

The cargo was a mixture of traded items that were so sought after back home, along with the remaining gold ducats, silver coins and various other gold coins, which had not been spent on trading, baksheesh for the local officials, or wages for the staff who had left Batavia a few days and weeks beforehand.

The VOC has closed their operations in the "spice islands" and this was the last shipment to leave the port. There was a smaller trading post in the east of the Javanese island where they would collect the last of their cargo and a further ten male passengers.

The trade winds were very sluggish at this time of year, so the going was slow as they headed east almost parallel to the coast.

After a further five days laying at anchor with barges travelling from the port to the ship and return, the Merkurius departed from Surabaya fully laden. It was heavy with the unspent gold, silver and the last of the VOC officials. This made the movement of the ship even more sluggish, and it sat extremely low in the water.

Over the last five years before the Dutch evacuated Batavia, four of the VOC ships were mysteriously lost at sea with no survivors.

These ships had been on a similar course to the Merkurius.

After many years, news leaked back to the Dutch colony that these ships may have been pirated by the Makassans, who had been a thorn in the side of the Dutch for many years, with several battles being fought and some lost.

The captain had just ordered a course change that would take them on a southerly course to pass between the islands of Bali and Java, so they could enter the eastern end of the Indian Ocean, when an approaching ship was spotted by the lookout.

The Makassan pirates approached the Merkurius flying the VOC flag upside down, showing that the crew was in distress. They caused the Merkurius to come within one hundred yards and then the pirates turned their ship broadside to the Merkurius and opened fire with their deck canons. The captain had been wary of the pirate's ship's movements and already had the crew closed up for action with half of his deck guns loaded. The Merkurius began returning fire soon after the first salvo hit the water just beyond the ship. The captain at once ordered all guns to be loaded and fire at will as they came to bear on the target.

The first salvo of shots to hit the Merkurius, took out four of the forward guns and their crews on the upper deck on the port side. The captain ordered a course change to face the enemy with his forward aimed guns and after fifteen minutes had completed the rotation to have all his starboard guns bearing.

By this time, the pirates ship was burning fiercely with all the sails either on fire or ripped to shreds. They now had no steering.

The Merkurius did not escape damage. Apart from the forward guns on the port side which were the first to suffer damage, a fire had broken out near the stern of the ship causing the steering gear that controls the rudder to be damaged.

Many of the crew were busy pumping water onto the fire but it could not be contained before they lost steering altogether.

The pirate ship was of no further threat to the Merkurius as it was on fire from bow to stern and all the masts were either on fire or laying at odd angles and of no use to the ship.

But the captain had much more on his mind. The ship was also taking water. One of the pirate's shots must have hit just on the waterline and had sprung several of the timbers causing them to leak.

Then one of the magazines which held the last of their gunpowder blew up.

This explosion destroyed most of the top deck amidships and set a raging fire in the hold and killing about half of the passengers and several of the crew.

Most of the rest of the crew were manning the hand operated bilge pumps which were now pumping water onto the fires. With a portion of the water being sent over the side through the scuppers, the threat of sinking had diminished.

A sudden gust of wind sent sparks forward to the bow of the ship where many of the remaining passengers and crew, who were not handling the bilge pumps had gathered. Someone had forgotten to remove the unused gunpowder from near the forward guns.

It exploded with such a force that it sent several the crew members over the side among the burning embers. Those who were left on the foredeck had been burnt in the raging fire.

But the remaining ten crew, egged on by the captain, fought feverishly with the pumps and after several hours, had the fires under control.

But they were exhausted, and they just lay down on the deck to recover, covered in soot and burns.

The fire fight lasted for about three hours with all sorts of horror being bestowed on each other.

With both ships having no steering, the current kept them moving in a southerly direction, away from the islands and out into open waters of the eastern Indian Ocean.

Chapter Two

The British were also remarkably busy trading around the East Indies and their presence was not welcomed by either the Makassans or the Dutch and there are several reports of conflicts between them.

HMS Vertigo, one of the Royal Navy's brigantines, was sailing west in the East Indian Ocean and just happened to come across these two severely damaged ships that were moving southward in close proximity and after not getting any response to their calls, went in for a closer look.

Both ships were almost destroyed above the waterline and the bodies of the crew were scattered all over what remained of the decks. There were no on-board fires, so this made their job a little easier.

A crew of ten men rowed across to the two ships in one of the longboats. They had the grizzly task of searching for any survivors of the drastic scene. They found that all the men on the smaller vessel, the one with no cargo and suspected of being a pirate vessel, had perished.

On the larger ship which still had the undamaged nameplate attached, turned out to be the "Merkurius." Of these crew, they were able to find only ten men who had survived the mayhem which had endured here two or three days prior to their arrival.

After an inspection of the two ships, the captain ordered the pirate ship, which had no cargo, be set alight, burnt, and sunk after the deceased crewmembers were all buried at sea. The dead men of the Merkurius were also buried at sea and the ten survivors were taken on board HMS Vertigo. Among these men was Captain Claus Herman DeJong but all were in an extremely poor state of health, all with burns to their bodies.

As the deceased crewmembers were all buried at sea, using the remnants of the sails and some of the unused shot as ballast, the captain spoke a few words and offered a prayer as they departed below the waves.

By mid-afternoon, a heavy line was attached to the Merkurius and it was taken in tow and with the long line the two ships made their way so very slowly south-eastward.

The skipper of the HMS Vertigo, Commander Kensington James Babington, Royal Navy, had not reckoned on having another ship in tow and the return trip back to England would not be possible.

The survivors were dealt with by the medical officer on board and was assisted by several of the ratings who had some medical experience. Four of the survivors died on the first night. Whilst they were doing everything that they could for the rest of the survivors, their injuries were quite severe and another five of them died before midday. It seems that it was only the captain who survived and that for only another week.

It was only a few days earlier that Commander Babington had charted a small island with a tall hill in the centre close to their present location and he altered course to head there.

This island did not appear on any of his charts, so he approached very cautiously as the tide in this area are about twenty-five feet variation from low to high.

The entrance to the safe harbour, up one of the wider creeks, was exceedingly difficult to navigate, so he anchored the Vertigo and the almost wrecked Merkurius just off the shore and his first officer and several of his crew examined the cargo, which seemed to be largely untouched by the fracas which had decimated the passengers, crew and almost destroyed the ship.

While the first officer and ratings were inspecting the Merkurius, Commander Babington was spending some time with the Dutch captain. The Merkurius' captain, Claus, was telling Babington about his dreams to help his wife in the growing of the tulips. They talked at length about the pirates' attack and how Claus had thought that he had done everything possible to minimise the damage to his crew and ship. But they concluded that all was done by Claus and his crew that could have been done.

That night, despite his care and best efforts by the medical officer, Captain Claus Herman DeJong succumbed to his injuries and passed away. He was the last of the Merkurius crew. Just as the sun rose next morning, he was given his last rites and taken from the ship by longboat and rowed well out to sea for his burial.

The cargo consisted of chests of trading items like spices, cloth, wood carvings, VOC company records and several very heavy chests, which upon opening, revealed strongboxes of gold, silver, coins, and some jewels.

As HMS Vertigo was a fast brigantine with a full complement of crew and Marines, there was little capacity for a large cargo.

Commander KJB had the heaviest of the cargo shipped to a convenient place at the edge of the tidal creek and stored. Much of the other cargo was loaded into spaces below decks of the HMS Vertigo for transport back to England.

The Vertigo laid at anchor beside the hulk of the Merkurius for two days, while the captain sent out a reconnoitring crew to find a safe passage through the exposed rocks to the larger tidal creek that was evident by the mangroves. The passage which they surveyed was a zig-zag course that was difficult to navigate. But by positioning the ship as close to the beginning of the course, the only option was to wait for the rising tide and with the help of a rowing crew in the longboats, the passage would be successful.

The Vertigo was towed by the crews rowing all four of its longboats along the creek and after two tidal changes finally had it moored in a suitable location and anchored so it would just remain afloat even at low tide.

Many of the crew were put back onto the Merkurius and worked for several days to try to make the ship seaworthy, fit a new mast and make a sail or two from the shreds that was available.

Commander Babington wanted to chart the island, so he sent out two of the longboats with full crews, to follow the coast of the island and map all of its features. He allowed them to also use their imagination to apply a few names to what they were able to.

While this work was being carried out, the captain and the first mate with a couple of the most trusted crew, set about locating a safe place to store the boxes which held the coins and bullion so they could return with a suitable ship to convey the load back to England if the refit of the Merkurius was unsuccessful.

The island was scouted for any location. They walked around just inside the mangrove belt and found several creeks. There was a forest in one section and a swamp in another, so neither of these would be any good. They found near the centre of the island, after rowing up to the extent of the tidal creek and working their way through the jungle that covered it, a hill. This is what Commander Babington has seen from a distance a week or so ago.

About a quarter of the way up the tall hill near the centre of the island is a cave. And after the bats had departed, they investigated this for a suitable location for them to store their treasure. Many yards into the cave, around a corner, lies a number of large boulders in a group. By carefully manoeuvring four or five of these rocks, they were able to create a hole into which the large crates would fit and then rolled some more large rocks on top of them, to hide them from prying eyes and keep it stationary should there be a king tide that reached that far.

Beside the river near where the Vertigo was moored, they had seen evidence of some local activity in the past, so some of the Makassan fisherman probably used this island as a short-term base. In several places there was evidence that cooking had taken place. Some scorched rocks and soil showed where some cooking fires had been used in the past.

One of the crew had been a master mason and with the help of a few others in the crew set about making a building out of the limestone rocks which were in abundance by the creek. When it was completed, a placard was made with the words "The Palace" carved into it.

After spending a week on the hulk, it was not going to be ready to sail any time soon. Using the same procedure as before, the hulk was towed by the rowers in the longboats into the creek and hauled part way up the low sloping bank. It would be high and dry at low tide.

Commander Babington took some time to make a map of the island, from the detail of the returning crews, renaming many of the points of interest for future reference. With some measuring and several star shots, he was able to confirm the location of the island. He was unsure if he could trust any of the crew, so he had his cabin boy, Tim, a lad of 10 years, assist him with this piece of the project. He was careful to not mention the location of the island in the ship's log but make a notation of it on the reverse side of the map which he had just completed.

When he had finished the map and he was satisfied that it was as accurate as he was able to have it, he had the boy carefully make a place to store and hide it, should the worst happen. Only he and the boy new of its existence and the hiding hole.

Chapter Three

The captain's telescope was two feet in length
and about three inches in diameter and fitted
snuggly into a double layered leather cylindrical
case. He was able to split the two layers of leather
and carefully fitting the rolled-up map in
between the two layers then reinserting the inner
section, thus creating a very safe place for the
map. He instructed the cabin boy to guard it with
his life and keep it stored in his own quarters
within the captain's cabin.

The order was given that on the next falling tide,
HMS Vertigo would set sail out of the creek and
head back to England.

The year was 1803, in the month of October.

Using the longboats to tug the Vertigo down the
creek on the falling tide, they were able to
navigate out of the creek, past the exposed rocks
by the entrance and headed out to sea.

After skirting a large storm to the south, they were forced to sail closer to the island of Sumba than the captain would have liked. After his discussions with the recently departed Merkurius captain, he became wary of the possibility of encountering pirates but they continued their westward journey without interruption.

The Cabin boy was a very clever young chap and he had spent many hours working with the ship's carpenter and sailmaker. He made himself a heavy-duty sea chest with several compartments into which he could store all his possessions. It was into this chest that he saved the telescope case.

Timothy Ignatius Merriweather was the name of the cabin boy who took charge of the telescope and sea chest, which he made in the carpenter's shop with the ship's carpenter. He was immensely proud of his handiwork and the ships carpenter, had at the time, commended him to the captain for his diligent handiwork. Tim's sea chest was very robust, made of solid oak with iron bands around the base and over the curved hinged lid to give it added strength. Rope handles were attached which would allow it to be managed. His sea-chest was lashed to the bulkhead and fitted beneath his hammock. To access the sea-chest he would fold away his hammock, untie the lashings which held it to the bulkhead and undo the latch to lift the lid.

On the third morning of their return trip, the weather was foggy and with little breeze with which to steer the ship.

From behind and off the starboard quarter the attack began.

The pirates were using another of the VOC's captured ships. This crew of pirates were very well versed in the art of naval warfare and were a very formidable enemy, even for the British. They did not carry lights and were almost invisible in the early morning fog. The Vertigo had its usual navigation lights ablaze as well as a masthead light. They would have been easy for the pirates to see in the dark. Even the midshipman in the crow's nest did not see the attacking ship until it appeared out of the fog.

The lightly loaded pirate's vessel was just two hundred yards astern of the Vertigo before it was spotted. With the light breeze and the heavily laden ship, there was not much in the way of manoeuvring that the crew could manage. The pirates were very soon abreast of them, and their cannons fired at a fast rate but with little accuracy.

The Vertigo crew were not sluggish at their task but the ship was overrun by the pirates after just an hour of fighting by cannon and musket. The pirate's ship came alongside the Vertigo and upon boarding tried bailing up the crew. Hand to hand combat continued for half an hour. The captain had fired both his pistols and killed two pirates. He handed the pistols to Tim to take them to be reloaded, while he continued to defend the ship with his sword and dagger. Tim headed for the cabin and at the last second noticed that he was being followed by one nasty looking pirate. Tim opened the cabin door and then very quickly took up a hiding place and filled his hand with one of the captain's spare cutlasses. As the pirate came through the door he was met with a very accurate blow from Tim's cutlass. His blow may not have been too powerful but it was accurate. The pirate was shortly lying dead on the deck.

Tim had the wit to not spend time on what had just happened as he quickly reloaded the pistols and ran them back to the captain.

The skirmish only lasted for a short while after he handed the pistols back to the captain and the remaining pirates fled over the side of the ship and swam back to their vessel. A few shots were fired after them from the deck cannons as parting shots.

At the age of ten years and nine months, Tim had been blooded. When he stopped to gather his thoughts while the big clean-up continued, he retched over the side.

The ship was damaged but after several hours of repairs, was able to get under way again, while more repairs were being carried out by the ship's carpenter and all hands.

By the nightfall on the next night, those who had been killed by the pirates were buried at sea and the sickbay held several of the crew being attended to by the medical officer.

During the return trip, the captain assembled the crew and during his address to them announced that Tim had been promoted to midshipman.

The rest of the trip back to England was uneventful.

In the little spare time that he had whilst on this return journey, Tim was also hand carving a replica model of the HMS Vertigo. But on this uneventful return trip back to Portsmouth he was able to put more time to this little project and by the time they sailed into port it was completed.

The ship was manoeuvred alongside the wharf and the unloading of the cargo began. Nets were used and lowered onto the deck and the cargo was loaded onto this net and lifted with the use of hand operated cranes to lift the bundle, swing it over the side and lower it to the wharf.

After the Captain had descended the catwalk, he was greeted by a Rear Admiral who had heard of the action in which they had been involved and needed to talk with him urgently. With his back to the workings, he did not see the loose heavy hook of the crane swing his way, before it collided with his head. It was a heavy blow which even the Rear Admiral did not see coming their way.

Commander Babington was knocked to the ground, suffering a fatal head injury. As he lay sprawled on the dock, several of the ship's officers raced to his side, hoping that they may be able to help but he was beyond any mortal help at this time.

All unloading work ceased as the crew gathered round their fallen skipper and officers, lamenting his departure.

Several days later, the funeral was attended by all the crew. At this sombre event Tim was pleasantly surprised that nobody had approached him about the map. He was quite sure that nobody else knew of its existence and he was keen to honour the captain's wish and keep it secret.

The crew had removed all their belongings from the ship as without their captain, they would not join the ship's crew for a week or so to show their respect for him.

Tim's uncle had a small farm just to the north of Portsmouth and he had his sea-chest delivered there by the carrier. His uncle had asked him to stay and help him on the farm, which Tim did agree to, for the time being, always knowing that he would return to sea at some point.

Milking the cow and shearing the sheep was a new experience for Tim, as was the mending of the old barn. Several of the roof timbers needed to be replaced and with Tim's carpentry skills, this was a task that he enjoyed.

After several weeks of farm work, Tim was called back to crew another ship for the King. The ship that he was crew on, was in convoy with trading vessels from England to Ireland during the union. Spanish and Portuguese ships had attacked several convoys and needed some armed protection.

He was promoted to Boatswain's mate at the closing of the journey. Tim is well liked by his peers and performs his duties, well above the requirements.

Before he could return to the farm, the French and Spanish navies got into trouble with the King's Royal Navy. Tim was assigned to the "Neptune" which was commanded by Captain Thomas Francis Fremantle. The battle which ensued took the navy ships under the control of Admiral Nelson into the Mediterranean Sea. It was a victory for the King's Royal Navy. Many of the sailors were injured and some killed but on the Neptune, they only suffered the loss of five men. The skirmish that they were involved in was the Battle of Trafalgar.

At the completion of this tour of duty, Tim returned to his uncle's farm. He noticed that the young lass from the farm next door, Dell Farm, was working from dawn to after dusk and he developed an affection for her. Just a few days after his twentieth birthday, he and Mary held their wedding ceremony in the local church. After the wedding they returned to his uncle's farm and continued their work as before, helping out on both farms. Tim's uncle was aging and slowing down and after a relatively minor accident he passed away. Because the farm was tenanted from the local Squire, they lost the farm. He and Mary moved to her father's farm and they continued running Dell Farm.

After several years Mary gave birth to a son whom they named Thomas after his captain from the "Neptune". Tim had been away from home for several months at a time while he was required on the ship. By the time of his son's birth, Tim was promoted to the rank of Boatswain.

Tim was required in the navy for the next fifteen years with the occasional return home for furloughs of a week or two at a time. During these trips he acquainted himself with the skills to navigate by sexton, compass and clock.

As young Tom grew up, he became very efficient at the farm work and he and his mother developed a good income from their dairy cows, selling milk, butter and cheese. The sheep produced some good wool and the pigs kept them in meat for the kitchen as well as some income from the local markets. They had a stall at the town square markets and they attended every week, selling their milk, cream, cheeses and meat. There was also a good market for their wool, amongst the local ladies.

Alice and her family who also had a local farm, had a stall nearby and after a courtship she and Tom became married in his twenty first year.

By this time, Tim had retired from the navy and he was able to spend time with his family and become to enjoy his time with them, even though it was a much quieter life than he had been used to in the navy.

Tom and Alice produce a grandson for Tim and he spent as much time as he could with the child and developing a sense of the navy in him. Young Tim was named after his grandfather and they also shared the same second name as was very common in that time.

Young Tim was a good student and learned fast. By the time he was six years old he could tie knots, read, and write. Before long he would help his grandfather working some wood and making items by his own hand with only supervision from his grandfather. Carving a copy of his grandfather's first ship, the "HMS Vertigo" was a favourite accomplishment of his.

Often you could see Tim and his grandfather down by the wharf, taking a look at the navy ships which came and went. Tim developed a good understanding of ships from his grandfather and he could not wait to get to sea himself. He had learnt the names of all of the parts of ships and the different types of ships. He knew a battle cruiser from a scow and a frigate from a longboat as well as their armaments. He could name all of the masts, sails and spars that were used on the ship and when they would be required to be ready for use. Old Tim's knowledge of navigation was also passed onto the younger Tim, although he did have some difficulty with some of the calculations.

Shortly after his tenth birthday, young Tim was enlisted on Her Majesty's Ship, the Vigilant, of the Royal Navy, which was captained by Commander Briggs and was bound for India and the spice islands of the East Indies.

His grandfather had told him of the contents of his old sea chest and about the map and how he could find it but said that he must not try to remove the map from its hiding place until he had acquired his twenty-one years of age. Tim was given the old sea chest to take with him on his sea journeys.

Old Tim had also written a letter of explanation to Tim and the heavy envelope had the tile of "To be opened on your twenty first Birthday". This was also enclosed into the sea chest.

He was a cabin boy, just like his grandfather before him and he soon set about his duties with diligence.

The convoy of five ships sailed southeast, just to the west of the coast of Africa, before heading northeast with the trade winds filling their sails.

The trade winds kept up a steady twenty knots and the ships made great headway for the first ten days.

One morning near thirteen degrees south of the equator, and about one hundred and seventeen degrees east, the convoy encountered a dead still condition and a misty morning. The mist was as thick as a London fog and the ships lost sight of each other. They were about to head in a northerly direction from this point to arrive at their port of call in India. After several days of being becalmed, a gentle southerly began to blow.

Due to some confusion over which ship was to turn first, the trailing ship collided with HMS Vigilant. The ship rocked badly and began to list. The crew checked all decks and the main damage was to the port side below water level and their fresh water supply. All but two barrels were split and leaking badly. Ropes and sailcloth were tied around the barrels in an attempt to stem the flow but little could be saved. The ship's carpenter and many of the crew began shoring up the damaged hull and after several hours the leakage had been stemmed and the handpumps removed the excess water from the bilge.

Now HMS Vigilant was seaworthy again but they only had sufficient drinking water for three days.

The weather had changed and there was high cloud travelling at speed and the captain was sure that this was an indication of a building southern hemisphere cyclone. The breeze had changed to a northerly and they would not be able to reach their destination. If this storm turned into a cyclone, it would be very early in the season, as they usually did not begin until closer to new year.

Commander Briggs was aware of several rivers which emptied into the sea from New Holland, which was discovered by William Dampier way back in 1699. He checked his charts of the area and decided to alter direction and head there to collect more fresh water. The ship's carpenter was made busy again now to build more barrels from what he could salvage from the broken barrels.

The winds had increased in velocity and the captain called for all but the foresail to be lowered and stowed away. The ship was secured for a storm.

The storm raged for several days and a lot of rainwater was collected. The problem was that the seas were so rough that all this new fresh water was tainted with sea water and was not suitable for drinking.

HMS Vigilant continued on a southerly course and Commander Briggs was concerned that he may reach the mainland before the storm subsided. But luck was with him and the storm abated and a soft westerly breeze began.

On the morning of the twenty fifth of October in the year of 1883, HMS Vigilant was anchored within a mile of the coast of this southern land, known as New Holland, where the water was stained a muddy brown. This was obviously where the river emptied into the sea. A longboat was launched and samples of the water were returned to the ship and it was deemed to be unsuitable for drinking. The longboat was sent to follow the stream inland to find a section of clean water which could be collected.

After several trips upstream, sufficient water was collected to fill all the freshwater barrels.

By the twenty seventh they were making ready for sea when the tsunami hit the ship from the northwest.

Chapter Four

The island of Krakatoa, in the Sunda Strait between Java and Sumatra, had been showing signs of volcanic activity for a few months with the intensity of these increasing as time continued. The captain and crew of HMS Vigilant were unaware of this activity as the trade winds were taking the smoke and ash away to the west.

In the afternoon of the twenty seventh of August, 1880, the island of Krakatoa exploded in one of the greatest volcanic eruptions for centuries. Two thirds of the island was blown away by the volcanic explosion and the sound of the explosion could be heard many thousands of miles away. But the sound of the explosion was not the only effect of the volcanic eruption. The movement of water around the island became explosive too and this created a massive tidal wave or tsunami.

That explosive sound followed the tsunami and reached the shores of where the HMS Vigilant was anchored. The tidal wave exceeded twenty-five feet and carried the ship up, over the closest beach and smashed it against the rocks of a low hill about a mile inland. The receding tsunami tide took the crew and much of the remaining ship with it out to sea, never to be found again.

At the time that the wave hit the ship, all hands were busy with repairs, most of them working above deck or over the side, suspended on ropes. The cabin boy, Tim was in his quarters. It seems that he was the only survivor.

Tim was injured but not even some abrasions and a broken arm would stop him from staying alive. He had seen the ship's doctor splint a man's arm before, and he was able to find the necessary sticks and binding to do the job. Tying the knots was difficult but by using his teeth he was able to get a fair knot to his bindings.

He survived those first few days beside the remains of the ship. None of the water or food that had been stored in the hold had survived the weight of that inrush of seawater and the smashing of the ship onto the rocks. He could not believe that he was the only survivor of that catastrophe. He had heard of giant waves before, but this was so much more than he could imagine.

After two days he began to wander along the creek, carefully tasting the water as he went. The sea water had destroyed so much and even caused the local river water to be salty. The further upstream he wandered, the less salty the water tasted. After searching for another two days, he found a supply of dirty, fresh water. He drank thirstily from this slowly flowing stream.

While he had been searching for water, he had seen some of the local wildlife. They looked so different from anything else that he had seen before. He had seen some deer in the woods, not far from his home, and of course the cows, sheep, pigs and horses on the farm back in England, but although the head of these animals looked similar to the deer, they hopped on their hind legs with their heavy tail held out behind. There were also some smaller animals like rabbits, but they were longer eared and had a blueish coloured fur.

After watching some of the animals for a while, he worked out a way to snare them with some of the vines he found growing nearby. He ate his first fresh meal without it being cooked. It felt good to have some food in the belly after all that time.

Tim wandered around the area where the HMS Vigilant had disintegrated on the rocks. There was still a small amount of timber which had not been washed away by the receding tsunami tide. These pieces had been lodged in between some of the rocks and he needed to work hard to remove them for his use. Several pieces of canvas were snared too, and he spent some time recovering these. One of the larger pieces was very difficult to remove as it was snared by the rocks and broken timber. As he removed the last piece that was holding the canvas down, it came away with such a rush that he fell over backwards. He winced with pain as his arm was still mending. As he stood up again, he was very surprised to see that his sea chest was laying there, jammed between the rocks. It had been covered by that larger piece of canvas and broken timber.

As he scouted around the area, he found a few tools from the carpenter's shop. He had also found a cast-iron pot, hammer, chisel, and a bowsaw. There was some damage to them, but he reckoned on fixing them up and putting them to good use. The few cannon that were scattered, as well as the shot, was of no value at this time, so he left them where they were.

He collected some of the timber and canvas and planned to go upstream where the fresh water was located and build himself a shelter. It didn't take him long to find a suitable location, which was situated some three miles inland from the wreck site and just off the creek on a high bank. His shelter which he built was rough, but he found it quite liveable.

He made a fish trap which he located in the tidal creek, and this provided him with a meal every few days. The snare that he set up had caught him another of the unusual creatures. They looked a bit funny but tasted okay when slowly roasted over the fire. He had taught himself to create fire with some of the hard stones which created a spark when banged together. The stones were very dark inside but coloured reddish brown on the outside. Much the same colour as the soil which surrounded him.

Chapter Five

On the north-western coast of Western Australia in 1867, brothers Roderick Mackay and Donald McDonald (Doddy)Mackay took up a tract of coastal country on the Yule River. Called Mundabullangana, the station was named for the aboriginal words for "End of Stone Country."

The base of operations for the Mackay's was just fifteen miles to the south-west of where Tim had set up his camp.

Neither knew of the others' existence.

It was several months after Tim's arrival, that one day whilst out trapping his furry meal, he came across a set of hoofprints in the hardening mud.

They were the hoofprints of a horse.

He had seen these back home on the farm too and began wondering if there may have been some other Englishmen close by. Tim became excited by the prospect of having some company after his dramatic ordeal. He would love to listen

43

to another voice as he was getting tired of talking to himself.

Even an argument with another person would be different.

He was able to follow the tracks for a few miles, but they disappeared when he came to some rocky outcrops, and they were no longer easy for him to find. He gave up for that day and returned to his camp.

He knew that for him to travel any further, he would need to carry a supply of water. He could go without food for a few days but not water. He had used some of the animal fat which he recovered from his cooking and had dressed some of his animal skins. By stitching some of the openings together, he was able to make them watertight. This gave him several bags with which he could carry enough water for a couple of days searching. It tasted a bit unusual, but it was clean fresh water.

Tim set out before daybreak with his three bags of fresh water. He went back to where he lost the tracks of the horse the few days before and he searched for them in a westerly direction, which is where he suspected that they were going. He stopped for a rest at midday, so he did not have to walk in the heat of the day. By mid-afternoon he reckoned he had covered about five miles, and the ground was very rocky, so the going was difficult. After his rest, he scouted around in a circle looking for any sign of hoofprints. But there were none. He kept on going until dark, keeping in a westerly direction. During the afternoon, the sun was square in his face, so he knew he was heading to the west. After the sun had set, it became too dark for him to see any sign, even if there was any to see. So, he set up camp for the night. He ate a little bit of his roasted bilby and drank half of his water before he went to sleep.

In the early morning, just before sunrise, Tim heard some noises outside his camp. He had not heard these noises for a long time, and it reminded him of back home in England. But after a few minutes he recognised the sound of lowing sheep and the dull sound of a sheep's bell. This woke him from his slumber and when he went out to investigate, he found some sheep about half a mile away from his camp.

Tim was quite sure that sheep were not native to this country, so they must be a sign of habitation in the area.

He gathered up the few items which he was carrying and headed out to the nearest rise. Once he got there, he looked out across the area to the east and to the south, where there was several hundred of these animals all grazing on the pasture. And towards the back of the group, he saw two horsemen.

He began walking slowly towards them so that he did not scare the sheep. He had walked about one mile before he noticed that one of the horsemen had turned and was heading towards him. He kept walking towards the horseman and the distance between them quickly became less. He was getting a bit excited too, at the prospect of meeting and talking with the man.

The closer he got to the horseman, he began to realise that this wasn't an Englishman on the horse but a man with very dark skin. Someone that he had never seen before. But the horse was of English origin with a saddle, bridal and other equipment that he had seen previously. The horseman reined-in about fifteen yards before he got to Tim and dismounted, leaving the reins of the horse dangling on the ground. He walked over to Tim in a bowlegged fashion as if he had been born to horse riding.

Tim had difficulty in understanding the words of the horse rider as he had never heard pidgin English before.

"Wot ya doin 'ere? Where come from?" were the questions that were asked of him in a barely understandable language.

But as he worked the words around in his mind, he reckoned that the black man was asking what he was doing here and from where had he come . After spending a few minutes deciphering the questions, he answered.

Tim tried to explain to the horsemen that he had been here for several months after his ship had been wrecked down on the coast. But the horsemen could not understand all the words that Tim was using and suggested that Tim should follow him back to where the base camp is. The horseman regained his horse and once in the saddle held out his hand for Tim. He grabbed the offered hand and swung up onto the horses back, behind the rider.

The black-skinned horsemen rode over to where the other black-skinned horseman was, minding their sheep and spoke quickly in another language that Tim could not understand. Then they headed off to the south-west by themselves, leaving the one horseman to mind the sheep. The horseman recognised that Tim was carrying water with him, so didn't offer him any. After about three hours of riding the horse, they reached the base camp. When Tim alighted, he was happy to see the face of an Englishman who was standing there to greet them.

The man extended his hand and they both shook hands in the usual greeting.

"Hello, there young man and what are you doing wandering around in this country?"

Tim was so excited to meet another person with whom he could talk, that his words would not come out for a minute or so, but eventually he began by telling the stranger of his last several months or so and what had brought him to this new land.

The man introduced himself as Sam Mackay and Tim told him of his full name, rank, and the ship from which he had come.

"You'd better come inside, Tim. You look like you could do with a good feed and a change of clothes."

Tim's clothes were a bit of a mess and had been torn several times but even with his sail stitching skills, they were a bit rough. Tim followed Mr Mackay into one of the bough shelters which they were using for their camp.

He instructed the cook to serve him up a meal of stew. Tim devoured this meal as though he had not had a satisfying meal for a month. A brew of strong black, sweet tea followed and shortly Tim became sleepy. Mr Mackay recognised the signs of exhaustion and suggested that Tim lay down on one of the bunks and have a rest. In just a few minutes, he was sound asleep. When Tim woke it was just after midday of the following day.

He had the best sleep since the tsunami had destroyed the HMS Vertigo, all those months ago.

He spent the rest of that day telling of his life and recent experiences and Mr Mackay listened with intent.

Tim was careful not to tell of the boxes of gold and silver which were hidden on that small island or the map that might lead them to it. He knew enough about human nature, that once that information got out, there would be a race to uncover the load.

Mr Mackay had never heard such a story, but he did know of the tsunami as they had lost a number of sheep that were closer to the seas' edge when it struck. He had also seen the damage to so much of his pasture, so he reckoned that the lad could not have made up such a yarn.

Mr Mackay invited Tim, to spend several days with the team while they sorted out what to do next. Tim asked if he could have a small wagon to go back to his camp and collect his most prized possessions. Tim drew up a small map of what he reckoned was the location of the wreck and his camp. It looked like he may have taken the long way around to reach these people.

To this request, Mr Mackay obliged and early the next morning Mr. Mackay hitched up a couple of horses to a light wagon and they headed off. Just the two of them. They took enough provisions for three days because even though there was a shorter track to where Tim's camp was, it still would take a full day to get there.

Chapter Six

The horses were very sure-footed and had been well trained in drawing a cart. It wandered around most of the rocky outcrops which littered the area but every now and then a wheel collided with a rock. Mostly they just bounced around in their seats but on one occasion, Tim was thrown from his seat. There was only bruising and after a short break in their journey, they continued onwards.

Around midday, Mackay called for a halt. They alighted from the cart and after collecting a few sticks from a nearby dried bush, MacKay built a small fire. Taking a black billycan from the back of the cart and some water from the container, which was carried in the cart, he continued to heat the water until it began to boil. Into this boiling water, he added a measure of tea and then some sugar. These items are stored in their leather pouches and carried in one of the boxes on the cart.

After putting the nosebags on the horses with a small amount of feed, they sat down on their haunches with their backs to the wheel of the cart while they drank their tea and ate some of the dried meat, which was part of the provisions as well.

After their grand luncheon break, they mounted the cart and got on their way again.

The river is divided around here, and they cross several of its tributaries. The sand caused them some problems but with their shoulders to the rear of the cart they made it through. The banks were not very steep, so this posed no problems for the horses.

Late in the afternoon, they arrived at Tim's camp. Everything was just as Tim had left it and he was pleased to see that his sea-chest was as it was supposed to be. He wouldn't open it until he was satisfied that he was by himself, back at the main camp.

The sea-chest and Tim's other belongings were loaded onto the cart but the sail which covered the camp was left intact and they made this their overnight camp.

The horses were unhitched from the cart and after the hobbles and bell were fitted to their front legs, they were set free to graze on some of the samphire grasses that abounded the area.

There was enough wood remaining, which Tim had collected for his fire before he left, so they made another fire to boil the water and provide a little warmth for the night.

Several hours after they had settled down in their bedrolls, Tim was awoken by the howling of an animal not far away from the camp. He had not heard that sound before and although not overly concerned was alarmed. Mackay awoke too and sensed that Tim was also awake.

"It's just one of the Dingoes that roam around here." He told Tim. "They won't hurt you but don't leave any food out or they will move in and steel it."

"I've not heard them before, and I was here by myself for about six months," Tim replied.

"Yes, they seem to move around with the seasons, but they don't bother the sheep too much, but we do lose a few."

The howling of the dingo seems to move around the camp, or maybe there is more than one animal out there.

The sounds drifted away as the dingoes became more distant and presently, the man and boy were back to sleep again.

Just before sunrise, Mackay was out poking the fire back to life.

Tim awoke to the smell of the fire and was out of his bedroll with his boots on before the billycan had boiled. A pan was heating by the fire and Tim had his first taste of oaten porridge for the first time in months.

"I never used to care much for this gruel," he told Mackay. "But this stuff tastes great."

"Best eat up, then we'll pack anything else that you want from here and we'll be on our way back to the main camp." Mackay told him.

"Can we go by where the "Vigilant" was wrecked, I reckon there will be more stuff that might be useful for us there too. It is only a few miles from here."

"Alright then, we'll make that detour and then we should be back at the main camp by nightfall."

Mackay headed off to find the hobbled horses. While he was locating the horses, he scouted around looking for the dingo tracks and by the sign on the ground reckoned on there being about five of the animals. The horses were easy to find as they were still grazing on the samphire grass and the bell around one's neck was ringing its dull note.

He returned with the horses, and they were both harnessed back into the shafts of the cart. The last of Tim's things were loaded on board and they headed off to the location of the last resting place of the Vertigo.

Mackay was astounded by what he saw. The site was at least twenty feet above the high-water mark and there were still some iron objects and pieces of timber scattered around, jammed in the rocks. Stuff that Tim didn't have a need for previously but would be useful for Mackay.

They scouted around and collected the larger pieces of timber, several iron objects but they didn't pick up any of the cannon. The cart was too small to carry such a load. If there became a need for them, he would later send out a heavier wagon and a team of men to collect them and anything that may be of value.

It was mid-morning before they departed and now that the cart was loaded, the poor old horses had to work a lot harder to drag it along the soft ground. The pace picked up as they moved onto the heavier ground and Mackay was more careful to guide the horses around the rocks. The creek crossings were more difficult and at one time they had to unload some of the stuff and carry it by hand across the creek and load it back on once the cart was on the other side.

The sun had set about two hours before they returned to the camp.

The cook greeted them and shortly had a meal served on the table.

While it was being prepared, the cart was unloaded with Tim's sea-chest being put beside his bed. He gave a sigh of relief as it was put down, as now all his possessions are back in one place again.

Those of the men who were around the camp seemed to show little interest in Tim's trunk or the rest of the timber and bits and pieces that were off loaded from the cart.

Tim thanked MacKay for recovering his worldly goods, bid him goodnight and went off to his bed for the night.

Chapter Seven

The work around the station was constant and MacKay was sure to make Tim fit in to whatever job was at hand.

With Tim's carpentry ability it soon became evident that he was very competent at the construction of buildings. He was able to build a new camp for the group who worked at the station.

With the workload and the increasing sheep numbers it was not long before the quarters for the workers became too small and additions were made.

The natives who worked on the station had their own accommodation by the river's edge where their tribe had their own camp.

Around the turn of the century, MacKay brought over from Isle of Skye in Scotland a stone mason and his son. The objective was to construct a new building as a homestead for the station. This would house the owner and his family. Several outbuildings would also be constructed as a cookhouse, mess hall and another for other staff quarters.

MacKay had himself emigrated as a young man from the Isle of Skye many years before and had known of the work which this stone mason had completed.

When Angus McKendry and his son Bertrand arrived at the station, they were pleased to see that there was an ample supply of raw materials for the construction of the buildings as requested by MacKay. He worked for a few days with MacKay, and they soon had some plans drawn up that they could follow.

The next few weeks were very busy with twenty men gathering rocks and stone that will be used for the buildings. A source of limestone was found, and this would be burnt to provide the mortar for the jointing of the rocks and stone to make a solid structure.

The building work commenced and at the same time Tim selected several men to assist him in sourcing some timber that would be suitable for the building of door frames, doors, benches and of course the roof. Most of what was needed was found about twenty miles inland where a grove of some larger gumtrees were growing. These were felled and sawn into suitable sizes before transporting back to the building site on wagons.

Tim had to employ some ingenuity as tools were in short supply.

MacKay had ordered to be sent up on board a supply vessel from down south, some corrugated iron that would be used for the rooves and some of the tools that would be needed to complete the job. When these arrived, the job proceeded much quicker. The homestead was completed after eleven months of work.

There was a break to the building work as shearing of the flock of sheep had to take place.

MacKay had managed to sort his flock into several different mobs, and these were mustered separately and shorn by the natives who turned out to be fairly good at the job. Tim took his place on the shearing board too and after a few weeks was doing just as well as some of the natives who had been doing it for years. When the older blokes saw how good he was, they too picked up speed and accuracy and the shearing was completed in record time.

To shear that number of sheep, it was necessary to have thirty men shearing at the same time, so the woolshed was extended to accommodate the greater numbers.

Hand shearing was used up until about nineteen twenty and Tim had become very proficient with the "blades." He was able to shear up to two hundred and eighty sheep per day but after about several years he found that his body could no longer do that amount of the strenuous work. He needed to find other work on the station that he was able to perform to his satisfaction.

At every opportunity, Tim would ride his horse over to the coast to where he was shipwrecked. He would always have a close connection to the sea but the work on the station is what he had to address his attention at the moment.

After this time, he would often ride out to the outstations with stores for the shepherds and then be found out in some of the far paddocks riding with the natives as they herded the sheep and kept the wild dogs away from them. He found that the best way to discourage the dogs was to shoot a few each week and leave their carcasses laying around for the other dogs to recognise. Although this did keep the dogs away for a while, after a few weeks a different mob of dogs would move into the area and begin killing and maiming the sheep once again.

During this period of time, Tim became very conversant with firearms. He got to learn how to dismantle, clean, oil and reassemble the rifles and handguns which were used in his days' work. He did take some time to learn the best methods to be able to shoot accurately and this would be of great advantage to him at a later time in his life.

He would take several weeks to visit the several outstations, and this took up much of his time. Mackay and Tim would travel out to the outstations and out-camps alternately, so they could each keep in touch with the men.

After the shearing was completed and all the wool was packed tightly into bales, they were loaded onto a wagon and driven down to the coast where a jetty had been constructed. The wagon was driven to the end of the jetty and the bales were loaded onto a lighter that would take the bales out to a waiting ship. It took several shiploads to move all of the wool from the station to the ports in England.

Because of his experience with ships, Tim was in charge of the operation of the two lighters. With an arrangement of ropes and cables attached to an offshore anchor, horses would drag on one end and when one lighter was going out the other was coming in. There were a few mishaps until they had the procedure figured out properly. But it turned out to be a very efficient method of moving the lighters.

After the completion of the homestead, McKendry the stone mason and his son moved into Port Hedland and continued with their building work in the new town.

Tim has been on the station, working for the MacKay family, for the last ten years and was tiring of the work and life's experience working in such an isolated location. Even now that Sam MacKay, nephew of the original owner was running the operations, things have changed and not for the better.

MacKay could see that Tim was unsettled and one evening they had a long discussion, and it was agreed that Tim should move on from the station. MacKay's other uncle was running a pearling fleet from Port Hedland and Tim began his next portion of his life back at sea, working on one of the pearling boats.

Tim left the station behind and headed his horse towards the town of Port Hedland. He had arranged to billet at the home of McKendry and his son, Bert. He constructed his own bed which was just high enough from the floor to store his sea chest beneath it. He was able to fit several screws to the bottom of the sea chest to fasten it to the floor. He fitted an extra latch and lock just to keep prying eyes from the contents.

McKendry had been busy with his building work and had several jobs going at the same time. He welcomed Tim and had him working with him on several of the jobs for a few weeks.

At the end of the day's work, Tim was at the harbour watching the pearling boats come ashore with their catch of pearl shell and always with a feed of fresh fish.

On Sundays he would spend time with some of the crews after having attended a church service in the mornings.

He did enjoy his carpentry work with McKendry but his heart was always on the sea.

Eventually by his nineteenth birthday he joined the crew of one of MacKay's pearling ships. The work was hard and the skipper was very tough on the pearlers. He stayed with the crew and worked his way to top deckhand within the year. Language was always a problem as there are Chinese, Malay, Makassans and Aboriginals on the crew as well as several English-speaking seamen. Tim learned just enough of each language to make sense of what was being said and how to relay the skipper's orders to them as they could understand.

All of the crew developed great respect for Tim and his attitude to them.

Chapter Eight

When the Mira was under sail, she was not the best-looking boat on the ocean or near the new harbour of Port Hedland but it was a rugged work boat and fit for its purpose.

The master of the ship had a very chequered past and was very hard on his crew and divers. The divers were paid to collect pearl shell and they were not allowed back on board the ship until they had a bag full of pearl shell.

Robert Blackstone or "Blacksie" claimed to have been a gunner's mate on board a Royal Navy ship which he claims foundered near the coast and had gone down with all hands. The story goes that he survived for more than a week on a makeshift raft. There were six men on the raft to begin with, just after the incident but eventually there was just the one occupant. There was never mention of what happened to the other men who shared the raft.

Blacksie claims to have had a hard time with a collision at sea, not long before the floundering of the ship with them nearly running out of drinking water. They had been collecting fresh water and were making ready to sail on the next tide when the ship was hit by a wave of the size he had never seen before.

The large wave had dashed the ship upon the rocks and washed the remains of the wrecked ship with its crew well out to sea. He never told of the name of the ship and much of what he recalled was very sketchy.

When he got drunk after the pearling season, he became very boisterous and aggressive. It was claimed that during an argument with several other men, he had killed one of them with his bare hands.

The Mira and the pearling company was owned by a Mr MacKay whose nephew operated Mundabullangana Station.

Young Tim had grown a beard by his twentieth birthday and Blacksie certainly did not recognise him and Tim only ever told Mackay of the shipwreck details. Tim who recognised him, was very wary of Blacksie and made a concerted effort to avoid him at all times.

But one night in the heat of summer, the pub was very busy with crews from many of the pearling boats and several arguments broke out. Blacksie was in the middle of a very boisterous fist fight which turned into a knife fight and spread out across the street. Tim just happened to be passing by and Blacksie, mistaking him for one of the fighters, lunged for him. But Tim had not been drinking and had the presence of mind to sidestep the onslaught of Blacksie. Blacksie faltered, turned around and lunged again and Tim was able to slip his foot in the front of Blacksie, tripping him up. He fell headlong onto the ground but the knife that was in his hand had buried itself into his chest. He died as he lay on the ground in front of the assembled seamen. When he went down, a great cheer arose for those who witnessed it and Tim was acclaimed as the one who had defeated Blacksie.

After a brief questioning by the local police Sergeant, Tim was found to be not guilty of the death of Blacksie and no charges were laid against him. Tim was free to go.

MacKay had noticed Tim's work on his pearling boat and employed him as skipper to replace Blacksie as skipper of the Mira. The crew had heard from the other boat's crew of how Tim worked with them and it was not too long before the catch increased with no extra expense. Tim was pleased with his crew's work and MacKay was pleased that Tim had become the best skipper in his fleet.

Tim was still unsettled even though he had good prospects in his current situation but he yearned to have his own boat.

Chapter Nine

Letter writing had been a task which Tim enjoyed.

Soon after his introduction to Mundabullangana Station, he wrote a letter to the British Admiralty to inform them of the loss of the ship, the captain and crew. In the same mail he also sent a letter back home to his parents, informing them of his plight and that he would be staying on in his present location for the time being and would let them know when that may change.

He also enjoyed receiving letters from home and with the current mail service, it was taking just three months from the time his letters were written until they were received back home.

He had been at Mundabullangana for five years when he received a letter from his mother advising that his grandfather had passed away. In the letter she also told him that he was the main beneficiary of his estate which amounted to one hundred and twenty pounds and this was held in the English, Scottish and Australian bank in his own name in Perth. A receipt was also enclosed so that he would be able to withdraw from that account but only in person.

Knowing that he had some finance behind him, Tim decided to leave that account to accrue interest until he had the opportunity to attend the bank.

That will be years away.

Just after his nineteenth birthday his mother's regular letter arrived, this time telling him that his father had passed away and after the selling of their farming estate, she had retired into Southampton. Her new house was a boarding house and she derived a substantial income from this.

All of his mother's letters were very carefully stored in his sea trunk with his other valuables including his grandfather's old King James bible, along with the telescope case that held Babington's Treasure Map which he was itching to open but refrained, as per his grandfather's request.

He was surprised that he had not received a letter from his mother by his twentieth birthday and had no response to those which he posted to her. There was no information regarding a delay with the postal service and he was anxious to understand the reason for this.

Some months later he did receive a package but from a solicitor in Southampton. As soon as he had the chance, he opened the package and it contained several documents and a covering letter.

His mother had passed away and the solicitor had been instructed to sell the boarding house after her demise. Along with the remaining investments from the sale of the farming estate several years prior, the funds were to be sent to Tim's bank account in Perth. The total of his inheritance from his family was five thousand five hundred and twenty-five pounds.

Tim was astounded by this amount and now was champing at the bit to carry out the next part of his adventurous life.

He was incredibly careful to not mention this fact to anybody in or around Port Hedland as there are many undesirable elements around who would gladly hit him on the head and take what was rightfully his. As he was still renting the room from Angus McKendry and his son Bertrand, he would not even mention the fact to them for fear of them letting slip at some stage. They did like their rum, down at the pub after work each day.

Early the next week he gave his notice to MacKay and agreed to work the week out. MacKay was not very happy and continually questioned Tim for a reason for his departure. All Tim was prepared to say was that his mother had died back in England and he had some loose ends to tie up. No amount of pressure from Mackay would make him change his story.

Angus and Bertrand McKendry helped him celebrate his twenty-first birthday a few days after his leaving MacKay's employ. It was a tawdry event but Tim refrained from getting drunk, as he was very careful not to let slip about his new situation or plans.

The next supply ship was due several weeks after he finished with the pearling boats and he booked a passage to Fremantle in a cabin. It cost him a month's pay for the journey but Tim was determined to make this trip solitarily.

Tim had seen these steam driven ships, complete with sails several times, as they arrived and departed with cargo and mail. But this was the first time that he had boarded a steam powered ship. The stench of oil and burning wood was heavy in the air as the boilers were stoked to build a head of steam for their departure. With a loud blast of the steam whistle, they set off on their southwards journey.

Once out to sea, the sails would be raised and much of the journey would be under sail. There were a few ports of call before he reached Fremantle as Cossack, Onslow, Carnarvon and Geraldton were also serviced by this supply ship.

Once Tim was satisfied that he had the cabin secured, he opened his sea-trunk and very carefully removed the lid of the telescope case. He withdrew the old brass telescope and was amazed at the wonderful condition of this ancient instrument. He carefully placed it next to his sextant in the sea-chest. Then after considerable difficulty, he carefully removed the map from the hiding place that had held it for the last eighty-two years.

It was still very legible and he was astounded by the detail that the old captain had gone to, to record so much detail of the island which held the treasure.

Even the colour appeared to not have faded.

But what was inscribed on the back of the map is what astounded him most.

In perfectly formed lettering was the following inscription…

KJB:

J22 30 5;

G14 4 1; G6 15 26; G17 12 5; G12 9 9

G6 3 25,26,27; G1 16 4; G5 10 11; G2 14 17

L11 19 14; G19 30 31; G35 8 12; E17 6 10.

Tim was aware of his grandfather's captain's name was Kensington James Babington and this created a great degree of consternation for Tim, as at this stage he was dumbfounded as what this code might represent. He copied this detail onto another sheet of new paper so that he could study it in detail. He then very carefully rolled the map again and returned it to its hiding place and after reinserting the telescope, stored the old telescope case back into his sea-trunk.

The ship kept just in sight of land as they journeyed along. Mostly under sails but they were furled and steam was used when the winds dropped off.

The new port of Cossack was the first port of call. Here they dropped anchor and several tenders brought out mail bags and a few crates which were stored in the hold. One mother and her two children boarded the boat also on their way to Fremantle. Several rather heavy crates were loaded on board as well.

When they anchored off Onslow, several sailboats arrived alongside to collect the mail and take off some cargo. Then a bag of mail was loaded on board along with several passengers who were also headed for Fremantle.

Carnarvon has plans to build a long jetty but that will be a few years away yet, but smaller low draft craft delivered mail and bales of wool to the ship while they remained anchored just offshore. By night fall, loading was completed and with that awful sound of the ship's whistle, they set sail once again.

At Geraldton, the Gregory Street jetty protrudes from the shoreline, into Champion Bay, just seaward of the main town. Many buildings surround the beach and the lighthouse stands prominent at the point. An overnight stay beside the jetty made a change from the heaving deck as they had endured since leaving Port Hedland. Tim longed for a hammock as it would have been so much more comfortable as the ship rolled with the movement of the sea.

While the unloading and loading of cargo while tied up at the jetty, Tim's eye was set on the boats that frequent the bay. Fishing boats of all sorts and sizes were coming and going. Departing early in the mornings and returning after midday. He could see that the majority were fishing boats and he wandered along the jetty to where several were tied up while they unloaded their catch of the day. The crews told him of their operation and the different sea conditions of the area. Mostly the boats were powered by sail only but several were also fitted with petrol engines that were used in the bay. Several of the smaller boats were man powered and the men operating them certainly looked powerful enough to row them. Mostly these men were immigrants from either Greece or Italy and fish in the same manner as they did in their homeland. Tim could see that this could be something which he could become involved in once he had settled things in Perth.

He had that urge to return to working on the sea.

The following morning the last of the cargo was loaded and that shrill whistle sounded again as they set sail once more, with Fremantle to be the next and final port of call.

Chapter Ten

Fremantle port is a busy place by comparison to the other ports they visited. The passengers were the first to disembark and as Tim departed the wharf area, he could see the cranes operating as they continued to unload the cargo and mail.

Tim had never travelled by train before and this trip from Fremantle to Perth was to be another new experience for him. The journey took just three hours as the train stopped frequently to service those passengers at the many stations along the route. He managed to secure his sea chest in the secure lockup at the station under the gaze of the grumpy old station master. He did like the five shillings which Tim gave him for his service, though.

Once he departed the train at the Perth station he walked the distance down to the main street and entered the bank by the main front door. He informed the teller who he was, showed his receipt and asked to talk with the bank manager.

In just a few minutes he was ushered into a lavish office and offered a well-padded leather armchair. He discussed with the manager his requests and a secure box was afforded him to store his most secret documents and items. He arranged for a few hundred pounds to be deposited into a bank account in Fremantle, so he could transact business without the need to travel to Perth each time he required some cash. The balance of his funds would remain with the bank and he was able to negotiate a suitable interest rate for a two-year period.

After leaving the bank, Tim wandered down to the Swan River and watched as the boats ply that water course. Some were heading west and others were going east and every now and then, one would travel to the south bank with passengers and a small amount of freight.

As he hadn't purchased a return ticket by rail back to Fremantle, he boarded a steam powered river vessel that was headed that way. As they travelled along between the riverbanks, he had a good look at the countryside along the river. There were some tall hills and some bends in the river and a few sand spits that the boat kept steering around.

Upon his arrival back at Fremantle, he found a rooming house for the night and settled in.

Next morning, he set about looking for a permanent address into which he could settle. From what he had seen of the area so far, it did remind him somewhat of Portsmouth but on a more spread-out scale and decided that this could be where he would settle.

If he planned to work on the sea, then to reside by the sea would be a sensible decision.

He visited with a land agent and had the option of several houses just to the south of the main township. One cottage closer to the seaside in Manning Street took his fancy. It had several bedrooms , good living quarters and an outside dunny. Behind the house was a laneway where the night-cart travelled to take the contents of the dunny each week.

He could easily walk the quarter mile to the harbour, which is where he expected to spend so much time. A price was settled at and after he had paid the asking price of £120/-/- and signed the necessary paperwork, he was able to begin moving in. There was some furniture already in the cottage and he soon acquired sufficient to put enough furniture in the house to make it his home.

After several days of wandering the fishing boat harbour and talking to many of the fishermen, he looked for a boat which he could purchase for his purpose of fishing. He was advised that perhaps he should work aboard one of the fishing boats before he purchased, just to make sure that he would fit in. He initially had some difficulty with the various languages that were used but he soon began to converse satisfactorily. He teamed up with Mario, who had arrived from Italy ten years prior and they spend several weeks working together. Tim arrived at the boat just before sunrise and they worked to the west of Rottnest Island for the day catching several different species of fish. They were stored in the hold which also held about a quarter ton of ice. The catch was unloaded back at the wharf and Tim was able to retire home before sunset.

The boat they used was a two masted, gaff rigged ketch, that was fitted with a small seven horsepower engine. It could be worked by one man but there was the safety margin of having that extra hand available and they also were able to increase the catch. And it was always good to have a mate around.

After several weeks, Mario helped Tim to look for the vessel that would suit him and after a few days of looking at the few that were available, he settled for a forty-foot boat, almost identical to Mario's two masted, gaff rigged ketch. It was soon out of the water and on the hardstand. Shortly Tim set about making it seaworthy and fitted it out to suit himself. He could handle all of the work except for that iron monster that took up so much room, smelled badly, but gave him propulsion. He engaged one of the local engineers to check out this piece of machinery and instruct him how to best use it. Mario had always been the one to attend to the engine when he worked for him.

The twin cylinder petrol engine produces seven horsepower and drives the forty-foot boat at 5five knots by a propellor attached to the end of a shaft which protrudes the transom. It took Tim several frustrating attempts to get the mongrel thing going on his first day in the water. He didn't usually use foul language but that mongrel engine taught him as many foul words as he had ever heard before. He did get used to it after a time and eventually it became his saviour.

Tim began his new life on the sea and was very efficient at the job of fishing. Several months later he learnt that some of the fishermen were catching the local lobsters and he set up his boat so that he too could participate in the venture. The crayfish, as they are known locally, are well sort after and they did return a good price if they were not sold through the official channels. Each night he would deliver his lobster catch to several neighbours, one of whom ran an eating house closer to the centre of town. He was always a good customer.

All summer he worked by himself and by the middle of autumn he needed to use his dreaded motor as the winds dropped off at that time of year.

One day he was motoring along between his favourite fishing spots when a southerly began to blow. He was of the practice that should he need to change over to sail power, he would leave the engine pushing the boat along. As he released the rope which would unfurl the sail, the rope became jammed at the top of the mast. The only way that this could be untangled was to climb the mast. This is something which he had done so many times, but never to correct a snagged rope, it was a great view from up there.

Tim untangled the rope but he forgot to tether the other end of the rope before he climbed the mast. The rope ran through his tough hands but broke the skin. The sudden pain took him by surprise and he lost his grip on the mast.

He began falling.

The twenty-foot fall was not interrupted by anything on his way down and he landed very awkwardly on the deck. His left leg was the first to touch down and the bones in his lower leg broke. Even as tough as he was, he let out an awful scream of pain. Unfortunately, there was no one around to hear his call.

The skin didn't appear to be broken but he could see where the broken ends of the bones were pressing on the skin. It was extremely painful. After a few minutes resting to regain his breath, he began to think of what he could do next, being twenty miles out to sea.

The boathook was close by.

He removed his shirt and tore it into strips. By binding the long handle of the boat hook to the outside of his leg with the strips of shirt, he tried standing without putting pressure on his broken leg. Even that exercise was very painful but he kept his head and made his way to the wheelhouse. By propping himself up against the sides of the wheelhouse and by standing on his good leg, he was able to steer the boat. He endured the pain and swung the boat around and pointed it in the direction of the harbour. It took 3 long hours to reach the port and because he was returning earlier than all the other boats, they were still out at sea. His only means of attracting attention was to constantly ring the big bell which was housed on the roof of the wheelhouse with a cord connected to the clanger that protruded into the wheelhouse. He continued ringing the bell until he hit the beach. Luckily he switched off the engine ten yards from the shoreline. The boat remained upright as the bow gently raised itself on the sand. Several bystanders could hear the ringing of the bell and ran to his assistance.

A stretcher was brought to the boat and after a policeman arrived, they were able to lift him over the gunnel and carried him to a waiting horse drawn wagon. The ride from the beach over the roads and track was quite rough and frequently Tim had to hold his tongue and not scream with the pain that he was feeling.

Fifteen minutes after he was loaded onto the wagon he was unloaded at the doctor's place. He was taken inside and after some initial treatment, the doctor gave him a piece of wood to bite down on, while he realigned his broken bones. Shortly a plaster cast was wound around his leg. He had to keep very still while the plaster set and he was glad of the piece of wood between his teeth.

He remained at the doctors for several hours.

Mario was one of the first fishermen to arrive back from fishing and was surprised to see Tim's boat away from the mooring and beached just off to the south. The policeman who had helped Tim to get to the doctors, recognised him and told him of Tim's problem. Knowing that Tim was well cared for, he got Tim's boat back to its mooring and unloaded his catch for him.

Tim was relocated to the hospital where he would need to spend the next few weeks while his broken bone healed. Tim didn't notice but the skin around the break was broken and the doctor was prepared for sepsis to set in.

He had never been inside a hospital before but was satisfied that this was the best place for him for the time being. He noticed that during the day, he was being cared for by a dark-haired nurse who always seemed to be very friendly. They got to know each other over the time that Tim was hospitalised.

Bethan had been a nurse for over five years and continued with a very pleasant bedside manner. It became obvious that she spent more time with Tim than the other patients and he was flattered by this attention.

After his release from hospital, he returned to his home and was needed to rest up for a further few weeks. He knew that the doctor knows best but he was itching to get back to sea. Bethan visited him at home just to check up on his progress, she said but after several visits he knew that there was more going on here.

Six months later, in October 1985, they became married with Mario being the best man.

They settled into their life together with Bethan working at the hospital and Tim continuing with his fishing. Now he worked just the five days a week, so he could spend more time at home with his beloved.

Within twelve months of their marriage, Bethan delivered twin boys for them. They were christened Charles and George.

Tim had returned to fishing again after he was fully recuperated from his accident and now walks with a significant limp and suffers pain in his leg when the weather changes.

Both Charles and George grow and Tim relates to them the stories which were told to him by his grandfather and helps them obtain a good insight into working on the sea. The boys are both very interested in great grandad's excursions in the Royal Navy from his early age to retirement. They were good students at school and spent time on the boat at every opportunity. They became good seamen and Tim was very proud that he had not just one but two boys, who may follow him in his chosen field.

It was during one very wet week that Tim decided to keep the boat on its moorings and spend some time at home with the boys, during a school break.

He had shown them the puzzle that he had rewritten from the Treasure Map of Commander Kensington James Babington, Royal Navy. The boys did have scripture lessons as part of their schooling and they reckoned that the initials on the document may relate to the King James Bible and not the old captain's initials.

Tim delved into his old sea chest and withdrew his grandfather's old bible from within. It was a first edition of the King James Bible and may well have been the one which the old captain had used to create the code. It was in surprisingly good condition, allowing for the fact that it had been stored there for around 100 years. He placed the heavy ancient bible on the table in front of the boys.

KJB:
J22 30 5;
G14 4 1; G6 15 26; G17 12 5; G12 9 9
G6 3 25,26,27; G1 16 4; G5 10 11; G2 14 17
L11 19 14; G19 30 31;G35 8 12; E17 6 10.

They immediately begin to search and presently they found the first clue.

If they looked in the book of Job, chapter 22, verse 30, word 5 they found the word, "Island".

The next clue was in the book of Genesis, chapter 14, verse 4, word 1 and found the word "Twelve".

Then looking in Genesis again but in chapter 6, verse 15, word 26 is "Fifty".

They kept on searching, becoming increasingly excited as they recognised more words that they were directed to by the code.

Shortly they had the island's location as 12 degrees, 58 minutes South and 122 degrees, 15 minutes East.

They kept at the puzzle until late in the night when they finally found the last of the puzzle. Bat, Cave, Under, Rock.

Tim had not shown them the map of the island and it took a while for him to bring the map back to memory. Yes, he remembered, there is a hill on the island and a cave which the old captain had named "Bat Cave".

They could hardly sleep but they had worn themselves out by using all of that brain power but were up early next morning and Tim suggested that they should be very careful not to tell anyone of what they had worked out. This secret had remained for about one hundred years and now was not the time to let anyone else into their secret.

The next item which involved their thinking was planning the trip to check out the treasure and a recovery mission.

Chapter Eleven

The rain continued to fall and this gave Tim and his teenage boys the chance to throw together some ideas of how they could tackle the next part of their situation.

They felt certain that they had solved the puzzle. Tim had produced a chart of the area from an old seaman who he had come to know and they carefully plotted the location of the island as the old captain had described.

12 degrees, 58 minutes South and 122 degrees, 15 minutes East, lies about five hundred nautical miles to the northeast of Port Hedland where Tim had been working on the station and then the pearling boats.

The fishing boat which Tim has, would be okay for the trip but it would need some alterations. They could remove the wheelhouse and construct a cabin with bunks and a galley. There are many other considerations too, but they will develop as their discussions continue.

Tim and the boys delved for hours over a sketch pad, compiling ideas that would need to be fitted to alter the boat to suit its new purpose.

They narrowed the ideas down to just those which Tim agreed to as he is the one with the experience of the sea.

As the weather fined up, they were able to trolley the boat from the water and arrange it on the hard stand, where they would be able to carry out the alterations. They became the bone of contention around the boat yard, as no one could remember an older fishing boat being transformed into a pleasure craft in such times. Tim and the boys were very careful not to divulge the real reason as to why the alterations were necessary. Tim just kept telling them, that he wanted his family to experience and develop a love of the sea.

By the end of the week, the old wheelhouse had been removed and the framework for the new cabin was completed. They worked from sunrise to sunset and by the end of the second week the new cabin was ready for its final fit-out with bunks and galley.

The engine was removed and replaced with a later model, which would produce fifteen horsepower and propel the craft along at ten knots with ease. There was also room to fit a larger fuel tank. The old compass, which is in its bracket just near the wheel, was checked by the local marine surveyor and only a minor adjustment was necessary. This would be a very important instrument in finding their island.

Four weeks after the boat was taken from the water, it was ready to be launched once again. Everyone was happy with the way it sat in the water and after a short trip out and around Rottnest Island, they were satisfied that their new boat was ready for the trip. The motor sent them from the berth to outside the harbour and they sailed around the island and back to the harbour again and motored back to their mooring. Prior to the relaunch, the boat was renamed the "Triple Tee".

The provisions were purchased and stored aboard and they were ready to head off.

Tim took Mario into his confidence and told him where they intended to go but not the reason for the trip. Saying that he just wanted to give his boys and wife, a taste of the old life which he so enjoyed.

Tim was careful to select the date of departure, as he did not want to be around the area of the island during the summer season which is locally known as "the wet". Usually during that time, the weather was hot and sultry with the chance of cyclones and heavy winds. So, to accommodate this they would need to be able to vacate the area by the middle of November.

Tim planned to sail into Geraldton, Carnarvon, Onslow and Port Hedland on the way to what they were now calling Babington's Island, so they would be able to collect any provisions that might be needed and make any modifications should they be necessary. The entire distance was about sixteen hundred nautical miles and if they average thirty-five nautical miles during daylight hours, they should be at the island with two months before they needed to depart the area.

With all of the attention that had been given to the refit that they had been doing, the cabin had been broken into one night. Tim arrived at the boat in the morning and knew immediately that something was wrong. The ladder which was usually lashed to the safety rail and leaned against the hull was laying on the ground. The latch on the cabin door was busted and someone had been inside rustling through the charts and moving things around. Obviously someone was seeking to find their destination but the charts of the waters above Port Hedland were still in safe keeping in the house. Although he could see that things were all shifted and their belongings had been rifled through, he could not see that anything was missing. The only damage was to the cabin lock. He didn't report the break-in to the police as nothing was stolen.

Tim had Bethan and the boys, Charlie and George, check out the cabin just to make sure that he had missed nothing but all seemed to be okay and ship-shape.

During the refit, Tim had built a cabinet that would safely house the telescope in its case. Another recess to house the sextant and keep it from becoming damaged should they hit rough weather. Luckily these were still in the house when the boat was broken into, so remained safe.

Tim was able to gather several of the charts that were necessary to navigate northwards up the coast and then northeast to the island. There was one chart that was missing that may have been an advantage but Tim was happy that he had enough charts to be able to safely navigate their way to Babington's Island.

By the middle of June, they set out on their epic journey, to find the island which held the treasure which Commander Kensington James Babington of the Royal Navy, had secreted away over one hundred years ago.

The trip to Geraldton was uneventful but trying, as they all had to work out the best way for all of them to work together. As there was four of them, they were able to change watch at the wheel every four hours. This would allow them a spell during the night as well as some daytime watch. The system that they worked out was great and they approached Geraldton a day before they had planned.

The fresh water was topped up but there were not any other provisions which needed to be purchased, so they spent the day spreading their legs as they walked around the town. Tim was surprised at the change in the town since he had been here those twenty years before.

There were sections of the west coast visible on good days as they sailed towards Carnarvon.

There was one section of the coast which had high cliffs with no chance of getting ashore safely there. Tim was careful not to head too far west, as the charts showed the Houtman Abrolhos Islands which were just off the coast.

Tim took the opportunity to teach the boys how to use the sextant on this section of the trip. He showed them that not only the compass was important to navigation but also the clock and a sun shot with the sextant during day light hours and a star shot during the night-time. After a few days they were each able to successfully plot their course, which was marked on the chart, along with the notations of the weather in the log.

They entered the Gascoyne River mouth at Carnarvon and dropped anchor in the bay. The dinghy was rowed ashore and they looked around the rough coastal town. The change from the ocean was appreciated by Bethan and the boys. The break from the continuous watches was a pleasure as they all made the adjustments while sailing. To have a solid footing was better than the heaving deck which they had not yet become used to.

They had been lucky with the weather so far as they only had a few rainsqualls and mostly with a breeze off the port beam. On one occasion they did have a storm but it only lasted during the daylight hours and they revelled in the sunset which lit up the western sky in a brilliant orange colour with black tinges to some of the clouds.

While they were ashore, Tim watched as a two masted schooner entered the river and dropped anchor downstream from the "Triple Tee". Something rankled in Tim's mind as he was quite certain that that same yacht was in Fremantle before they departed and again in Geraldton. It seemed to him to be a coincidence that they should be sailing on the same course.

He mentioned his concerns to the others.

Tim didn't think that there was anything to his suspicion but they did need to be wary of who they spoke to and what they should say, just in case there was something sinister about the intentions of those on the yacht.

They stayed two nights at anchor in the Gascoyne River mouth at Carnarvon.

The night before they departed Carnarvon, they had a discussion about their safety should they be attacked by another party. Although they were all against the use of firearms and killing people, the decision was made that while they had the opportunity, they should purchase a couple of revolvers.

Early the next morning, Tim rowed the dinghy to the shore and made his way to the storehouse. The storehouse supplies everything which the pastoralists require from here and guns was one of the items which they do sell. Tim carefully selected a pair of Webley .455 revolvers, each of which had a six-shot cylinder. He was conversant with this firearm, as he had the use of one of them while at the station.

Because they would need to learn how to use these firearms, they would need to have some practice, so he also purchased two thousand rounds of ammunition. It seemed a lot but there were not many places where they could resupply their ammunition should that be necessary.

Immediately after Tim had rowed back to the boat, they lashed the dinghy to its davit, weighed anchor and then motored to the mouth of the Gascoyne River. After setting the sails, they took a northerly course, keeping about ten miles from the coast.

Chapter Twelve

When the refit of Tim's fishing boat was under way, a bracket was added to the sail gaff jaws of the aft mast, so that when one of them climbed the mast, there was a foothold for them. With a special harness which the boys made, they were able to climb the mast, position themselves close to the top of the mast and use this as a lookout. The larger ships use a "crows' nest" but this was not an option for this smaller craft.

Charlie climbed the mast after they had cleared the mouth of the Gascoyne River and kept watch for the schooner, to see if it was going to follow. Just before the horizon blocked the view of the river mouth and the mangroves, he could see the triangle sail of the schooner as it left the river mouth. They maintained their course and the schooner followed them and it kept its distance, so that Charlie could just see the headsail as they rose on the swell. George took the lookout after several hours and just before dark, he was still able to see that headsail of the schooner keeping the same distance and course.

As they enjoyed their evening meal, they discussed what they could do and agreed that if they were to change course after dark and head west for two hours without their navigational lights, then before daylight double back and return to their previous course next morning, they should then be behind the schooner.

This action was taken and in the morning there was no sign of the schooner either ahead, abeam, or astern of them.

It was time that they all became conversant with the firearms which Tim had just purchased. When Tim purchased the two revolvers from the store in Carnarvon, he also bought a wooden box in which to house them. The extra ammunition was stored in another container by his bunk. Included with the purchase was a set of printed instructions of the parts, how to maintain the weapons and how to use them.

When Tim was on the station, he had full use of rifles and handguns and was aware of these things but he needed to make sure that each of the others was conversant and efficient with their use as well. He showed them how to clean and maintain the guns. He loaded 6 rounds into the cylinder and taking aim over the stern, fired off all shots. The two boys and Bethan were surprised at the sound and loudness of the shots. Tim ejected the shells and had each of them practice the loading of the cylinder with the spent shells.

The original course was resumed until they approached the cape to the northwest of the mainland. From here they sailed due east for several days with their course set for Onslow. Because of the many islands which lie close to the mainland, Tim elected to run about thirty miles off and parallel to the coast.

They recovered a few pieces of floating tree and by removing a section, the boys made a target which could be towed behind the boat. Each of them took it in turns to load, prepare, aim and fire the pistols and see who could hit the target the greater number of times. The boys were very accurate, as was Tim and even Bethan showed good promise. After the practice sessions, the guns were cleaned and stored back into their container, with the hope that they would never need to be used in conflict.

Barrow Island is well marked on his chart and having moored there in the lee of the breeze for several days, they were ready to head off in the morning.

During the last evening, the boys spend a few hours diving and caught sufficient fish for the next few days. The water here was crystal clear with about thirty feet visibility. They also collected a few pearl oysters and Tim spent some time explaining the many details of the pearling industry and about the pearl shell and its uses. They watched as an old sea turtle surfaced close to their boat. After it filled its lungs with air, it dived again, closely followed by the boys who swam alongside the old turtle for half an hour, before returning to the boat.

They skirted around several other small islands and set their course for Onslow.

The twins rowed ashore at Onslow, filling a few barrels with fresh water and returning to the Triple Tee. There were several other boats at anchor just off the coast and another few in the creek but the schooner that they were interested in, was not amongst them. It seemed to them that their manoeuvre the other night may have paid off.

They remained at anchor till the next morning and used the sails to depart. There was plenty of open water here and no obstacles, so the motor was not required and with a 5-knot tail wind, they set course for Port Hedland, keeping thirty miles from the shore. Those little low islands would be difficult to see while they sailed during the night, theirty miles would keep them clear. Those five days were very eventful for the family. They saw several whales each day as they sailed along. They found that if they kept their noise to a minimum, the whales would swim closer to their boat. The boys dived with one of the fat whales and it turned away from them. They were traveling at a similar speed and followed the whale all day, only to see her give birth to a calf in the afternoon. The boys took it in turn to view them from their lookout atop the mast and kept a running commentary to those back on the deck.

Another time, Bethan was startled when a flying fish landed on the deck at her feet. After her initial scream, she gathered her thoughts and prepared the two-foot-long fish for their meal. She did notice that a small shark was chasing a school of the fish and that may have caused it to leap so high.

Port Hedland in 1911 was so much different to the place which Tim had left so many years ago. They sailed into one of the tidal creeks and made

109

their vessel fast to one of the jetties which had been built. Leaving the others to mind the boat, Tim headed off into the main town and soon arrived at the house of Angus McKendry and his son Bertrand. He was greeted by a lady who turned out to be the wife of Bertrand. Bert was due back from his building project shortly and she invited Tim to wait inside. She told him that old Angus had passed away about ten years ago and Bert was now running the building company. He could see that the place showed that of a woman's touch, much like his was at home in Fremantle. Bert was surprised to see Tim and greeted him warmly. Tim invited them to come down to the boat and visit his family, having told them that he was not inclined to leave the vessel unattended.

They made their way to the boat and all introductions were completed. Their reunion continued into the small hours of the next day. Each explained their activities over the years, since Tim had departed.

Chapter Thirteen

The schooner which has been following the "Triple Tee" is named the "Pembroke" and is owned and skippered by one Englishman, Ted Dankworth.

It turns out that Ted's grandfather was Lieutenant William Edward Dankworth of the Royal Navy. Dankworth was the second in command to Commander Kensington James Babington aboard the HMS Vertigo.

Dankworth kept his own journal of the trip on board the Vertigo, which encountered the pirates and the Dutch ship the "Merkurius", transferred her cargo and buried a few boxes on an island somewhere south of Java.

He had his suspicions but didn't know the exact contents of the boxes but recorded that they were heavy and must have been valuable.

Because the old skipper died just as they arrive back in port, he had several suspicions and these also included that possibly the little cabin boy may know something about the secreting of these boxes and possibly what they contained but more importantly what was the exact location of the island in which they were buried.

The old journal noted that the captain had a crew who spent considerable time mapping the island and reckoned that this detail must have been recorded by the captain.

The location of that map was of prime importance to Ted Dankworth as he was sure that the boxes may hold many thousands of pounds worth of gold and such. Because of his connection with the ship HMS Vertigo, he reckoned that he was entitled to a share in its bounty.

When the "Vertigo" docked in Portland and the skipper was killed on the wharf, his grandfather spent the next few weeks onshore and become married. The son from this marriage was his father who also spent time in the Royal Navy. While he was absent, Ted spent a lot of time with his grandfather who related so many stories to him. Some of these yarns turned out to be fabrications but this one story stuck in the young mind of Ted and he was determined to track that little cabin boy and try and become involved in the recovery of this treasure.

Being a few years older than Tim, he did know that he was aboard the HMS Vigilant when it went mysteriously missing in 1883.

Several of the London newspapers of the time, reported that the ship had been lost with all hands. A year later they reported again, this time that the Admiralty had notified them, that there was at least one survivor from that wreck but they did not report on who it was or their whereabouts.

The "Pembroke", the skipper and the crewman, Finnegan, had spent a lot of time cruising the area south of Java in the hope that they might stumble upon the island. His grandfather had recorded some detail of its appearance but he was neither navigator nor a map maker but did make a sketch while they were laying offshore of the island.

Unfortunately, when the tidal wave may have hit the island back in 1883, many of the island's features could have changed. Even if he did stumble upon the correct island, it was unrecognisable from the sketch which his grandfather had made.

The schooner "Pembroke" stumbled into Port Hedland where they needed to reprovision their food and water supply. Ted and Finnegan spent some time talking with the locals and their ears pricked up when they heard the story of that ruffian, Blacksie and his claims of being from a ship that went down during that tsunami in 1883. The most astounding part of that story was that of a young bloke by the name of Tim, who is claimed to have killed Blacksie in a brawl.

Ted also knew that the bloke he was following was named Tim.

This must be the connection that he needed. He learned from the locals that Tim had left here about twenty years ago but none of them knew where he went.

Feeling certain that he was on the right track, they tried several other locations close to Port Hedland, both north and south but to no avail.

No one had heard of Tim Merriweather.

They sailed south and after trying in Onslow, Carnarvon and Geraldton, they continued onto

Fremantle and found a suitable mooring. The "Pembroke" skipper and crewman asked a lot of questions and became aware of a fishing boat that was being refitted with a cabin as if it was being readied for cruising.

They kept a watch from a distance and Ted was sure that this was the Tim Meriweather that he had been searching for. Now he had a wife and two sons who joined him with the refit and the subsequent relaunch of the ketch.

Ted was of the opinion that the family had all the information that was required to find the island and recover the treasure. He intended not to get too close to them or reveal his intentions but to shadow them on their way to their destination.

By keeping the top of the sails of the Triple Tee just visible ahead of them, the Pembroke kept an almost invisible distance behind the ketch. They waited offshore while the Triple Tee entered the port at Geraldton and tried to keep their distance again as they sailed northwards. At Carnarvon they did enter the river mouth and moored a distance from the Triple Tee while keeping a watch on the others all of the time. They saw Tim row ashore the following morning and return with several boxes of supplies. They delayed their departure waiting for the Triple Tee to complete about twenty miles.

Upon leaving the Gascoyne River mouth at Carnarvon, they spotted the Triple Tee well ahead of them and maintained that distance from them, keeping on the same heading, shadowing them until dark.

Ted was very surprised that by next morning they were not able to see the Triple Tee ahead of them. They furled the sails and drifted for a few hours in the hope that they may have overtaken the ketch during the night. After that time the sails were raised again and they continued on the northwards course and altered their course and headed eastwards as they came close to that northwest cape of the mainland. There are many islands on that next stretch of coast and they visited each one in turn to search for sign of the ketch. But all to no avail, they must be well ahead by now.

Little did he know but the ketch was in fact behind them and sailing at a leisurely pace. The schooner was faster than the ketch and this distance became greater with each hour that they sailed. The visiting of each of those small islands was taking time but these were closer to the mainland than where the ketch was sailing.

When the Triple Tee was moored at Barrow Island and enjoying a little break from sailing, the schooner sailed past them, but thirty miles to the southeast and neither saw the other.

Several days later, the schooner entered one of the tidal creeks at Port Hedland. They were not surprised that there was no sign of the ketch but there were a lot of boats about that size moored at different locations within a ten-mile radius of their position.

They waited for two days before they watched the ketch approach. Now that their sails were furled and the flag removed for the masthead, it would be difficult for Tim and his family to notice them amongst the other craft.

Now that Ted knew where the Triple Tee was moored, they could keep an eye on the activities of the family and work out their next move. He was against having a physical conflict with them but sometimes when men get desperate, things seem to take their own course.

Chapter Fourteen

Later, in the day following their reunion with Bert, Tim limped over towards Bert's house. His leg was giving him grief today from his accident seventeen years ago, when he fell from the mast.

It was just a mile and on the way he was approached by a man he had not seen before but who greeted him with his name and said that he was Ted Dankworth and that they had something in common that they should discuss. The pub was open for business and as they were close to it, they decided that this could be a good place for a discussion.

Ted asked Tim if his grandfather had been aboard the HMS Vertigo under the command of Commander Babington. Tim was astounded that someone else should be acquainted with his grandfather's situation, because he had never discussed this with anyone, even Mr MacKay, back on Mundabullangana Station. MacKay knew of Tim's situation but not that of his grandfather's.

Tim realised that Ted did in fact know some of the details regarding the Vertigo and the Vigilant and was therefore very careful not to divulge any further information, except to agree that the details which Ted knew were in fact correct, as far as they went.

When Ted mentioned that he believed that Babington had buried some Dutch treasure on an island not far from here, Tim did not reveal any knowledge of the fact and confirmed again to Ted that he was sailing with his family to have them discover life at sea.

Ted revealed that it was his schooner which had followed them from Fremantle and was at a loss as to know how they become separated on the leg of the journey, north of Carnarvon. Tim was beginning to become suspicious of this chap and quietly made his excuses and left him at the pub while he continued his journey to Bert's home.

Bert knew of Tim's experience aboard the Vigilant but not of his grandfather's involvement with the Vertigo. He spent some time with Bert asking all sorts of questions about the locals but Bert was unable to fill him in on many details, except that a few months ago, a couple of blokes were asking questions around town and they seemed to grasp the story of Tim and his altercation with Blacksie and that man's demise.

Tim was sure that those two blokes were Ted and his mate and this made him more suspicious. He told Bert that he would be sailing for the next couple of months and intended to return to Port Hedland and visit him again on their return voyage. He asked Bert to respect his decision for not telling him the true nature of this journey.

Tim told Bert about the altercation with the two men from the schooner and asked Bert to do him a favour and borrow a local boat and sail alongside them as they leave the creek and head out to sea. He reckoned that if the others could see two boats head out together, they might have second thoughts about following them. Bert, who had been sailing for a number of years, agreed to Tim's request for help.

If there were any developments after they separated in a couple of days, they could relay the details to each other upon their return.

Tim returned to the ketch and informed the family of what had transpired since he took his walk today. They were all taken aback to know that someone else was searching for what they were but with very limited information.

The map, which Babington drew up is still in a safe place on board and he confirmed that it should stay secret from anybody who should venture onto or into their boat. Tim had not marked his chart with the island's location and now has its reference firmly stored in his memory.

It only took Bert a day to get himself organised and had two of his working men crew for him for a few days. They thought it would be great to get away from the building project for a change and agreed willingly.

Around midday they sailed from the mouth of the creek, after first having motored down to the mouth. Tim set a course of due north as this may also give the schooner's crew the opinion that their destination lies in that direction.

The two boats could have been built in the same boatyard but the Triple Tee's masts were five feet taller and had a larger sail area. But both were ketches and gaff rigged. They sailed half a mile abreast of each other until nightfall, then Bert's borrowed boat fell in astern of the Triple Tee and they sailed in this manner, keeping a close watch on each other's location till daylight, when they sailed abreast again.

They kept up this practice for two days and made good headway and the weather was kind with a ten-knot breeze from astern. The swell was rising and Tim was concerned that this may indicate some rough weather approaching.

They kept a sharp lookout for the schooner but there had not been any sightings of it since they departed the mouth of the creek in Port Hedland. The rising swell gave them the chance to see a few miles further but still no sightings.

Before the third night, Tim pulled up close to Bert's boat and suggested that after dark, they should carefully alter course to the east and that Bert should depart just on sunrise and return to his home port by altering his course several times to approach his creek from the south. If anyone was watching, they would have little idea of the course that they had taken.

Bert noted upon his return to his mooring, that the schooner which Tim had identified several days earlier was not at its mooring or anywhere else to be seen in the area. He quietly asked a few questions around the place but it seemed that no one had seen the schooner depart. It was there in the afternoon, someone told him but by the morning it had departed. He told a few of his acquaintances that he had spent some time with Tim and his family and was glad to have caught up with them and renewed his friendship with Tim. They both were hard workers and had a great respect for each other.

Several days later, news came to him that Ted Dankworth and his schooner had in fact departed just on night fall of the day after he and Tim had departed, so he was satisfied that Tim would be safe from the interference of Dankworth.

He and his workmen returned to their work on the various building sites that he was in charge of but his mind kept wandering back to the fact that Tim didn't take him into his confidence regarding their destination. He was not overly concerned as he knew Tim would have a very good explanation for this upon his return. He just trusted that whatever they were doing, that they would keep safe.

Chapter Fifteen

Ted Dankworth and his crewman, Finnigan, watched as Tim and Bert sailed away from the coast at Port Hedland. It seemed unusual to Ted that Tim should have another boat travel with him but then again one cannot read another man's mind.

This got Ted to thinking that perhaps Tim felt threatened by his intervention with him yesterday, when they had that discussion at the pub. He certainly did not seem to take to Ted well at all and ended their meeting abruptly.

Ted had the notion that that may have been his last opportunity to have a share of what was reported by his grandfather. Perhaps there is no treasure buried out here anyway. Perhaps the old man was dreaming. He just wasn't sure anymore. Perhaps he had just been following a pipedream of his grandfather's. Maybe there is not even a map or location anyway. He was despondent but there was always that niggle at the back of his mind that there might be more to Tim Merriweather's excursion than he is letting on. Well, he thought, that seems to be the end of that saga.

Ted had heard of several stories about the tidal changes out near Ashmore Island which is about five hundred and fifty miles northeast of Port Hedland and wondered if Tim and his mate, were heading out in that direction, so he could show his family some more of the nature of the sea. With a thirty-foot tidal variation, the reefs which are there, are exposed at low tide and Ted would like to have the experience of viewing this phenomenon himself.

After preparing the Pembroke, Ted and Finnigan sailed off to the northwest in the direction of Ashmore Island.

Their first few days of plain sailing were interrupted with a following storm which had them furl the sails and just use the forward jib to maintain steerage and direction.

After several days of the heavy weather, the storm abated and they were able to make good headway again in the direction of Ashmore.

It was low tide by the time that they reached the exposed reefs of Ashmore Island and the seawater was cascading over the edge of the reef and draining back into the ocean in what looked like the world's widest waterfall. By the time they arrived, the reef was exposed by about ten feet. Had they sailed at night in this area, they would most likely collide with these exposed reefs at low tide. At high tide of course, they were covered by more than three fathoms of water.

After watching the phenomenon and sailing around the southern perimeter of the reef, they set a course that would take them around the island and look at it from the east. Ted was unwilling to sail around here during the dark, so they located a place just offshore and dropped anchor.

Next morning with a light westerly breeze, Finnigan carried out his normal duty by climbing the mast and search the horizon to make certain that they were alone or to identify any vessels which may be nearby. There was a boat approaching them from the east and its sails were badly shredded and it looked like the craft was in trouble. He yelled down to Ted, "Sails Ho! At six o'clock". He scaled down the mast and collected the telescope. Upon his return to the lookout, he could have a better look at the approaching vessel which seemed to be wallowing in the light swell. It was still several miles away but was heading directly for them.

Ted prepared the boat so that others could come aboard should they be injured or such.

The three men on the approaching boat looked as though they had been attacked as their clothing was torn and they looked like they in need of water and a good feed.

With just fifty yards separating the two craft, the newcomers called out in broken English for help. Ted waved to them indicating that they could come alongside and this they did. Because the boat was in such a damaged condition, Ted wouldn't let them tie onto the Pembroke in fear that should the other boat sink, it would drag the Pembroke down with it.

The three men immediately scrambled over to the Pembroke. They were in a very decrepit state of dress and one of them had a badly dressed wound to his upper leg. They obviously did need a feed but the water was offered first and they drank freely from the jug that was given to them.

They told a story of how they had escaped from a German ship that had taken prisoners to work on the plantations in the German held islands to the east.

The three men had been living on Celebes Island with their families in a mission and this is where they had learnt some of the English language.

They had been badly treated by the Germans and they found this abandoned boat and set sail back to their homeland but they were badly provisioned and needed to find some water.

Ted and Finnigan both noticed that each of the men were carrying knives in their belts and tried their best to remain calm. As the conversation progressed, the Makassans slowly became more aggressive and Finnigan took exception to the manner in which he and Ted were being addressed.

With the flash of a blade, Finnigan was stabbed in the belly and he doubled over with the sudden pain and disbelief that that could happen. He fell to the deck and one of the others heaved him over the side of the vessel. Ted tried to interfere and was stabbed in the side for his trouble.

The Makassans pirates took charge of the Pembroke and allowed the other craft to sink and they sailed off to the west. By next morning the other man who was injured died and he too was heaved over the side. Ted could see that he would get no compassion from these men.

Two days later he heard one of them yell out that he had seen the sails of a boat ahead and they altered direction to intercept. As they approached the vessel, Ted had no knowledge that it was Tim's boat that they were headed for. He tried to yell out but was tackled to the deck and gagged and bound.

Just the way that Tim had found him.

Chapter Sixteen

Tim's prediction of a change of weather was accurate. They had a following storm which would have given them the opportunity to make good headway but the seas became rough and they shortened the sails and sailed along at a rough 10 knots. The wind was blowing at about thirty knots with a twenty-foot swell and five-foot seas. They had everything lashed down and stored, just as the storm approached. The boat pitched, rolled, rose and fell and it became a most unpleasant trip. Tim had everyone who was not at the wheel to get themselves down to the lowest point in the boat that they could. This would reduce their centre of gravity and make the vessel as steady as possible.

With weather of this nature, there would be no galley to cook their food, so they had to rely on some of the biscuits which Bethan had baked prior to their departure from Fremantle. The oatmeal biscuits were laced with honey and she had to stop the boys from filling their stomachs with them. She did call them gluttons at one stage. Unfortunately, some of what they had eaten, had ended up over the side, in the ocean as they faced downwind at the critical time. There was no need to clean the deck though, as the rough ocean was doing that job for them too.

The storm raged for two days and petered out slowly.

There were just a few times when Tim was able to take a sun shot with the sextant, so that he could determine their location and he was satisfied that with just two more days of sailing, they should arrive at the island, which held the treasure as promised by Commander Babington's map.

Just a day out from their destination, with George at the mast top lookout, he yelled out to the deck below, "Sails Ho! At one o'clock", pointing to the afore starboard. Surely this could not possibly be the schooner that they had taken such pains to avoid. Tim immediately turned to port and headed northwards again, hoping to either outrun the schooner or draw it away from their destination.

He held this course for a full day but was careful not to hold it for any longer as he was approaching some of the Indonesian islands, and he was sure that some of their inhabitants were not all that friendly to foreign boats entering their waters. There have been reports that several of these islands were inhabited by groups of cannibals. Also, the German army has control of several islands to the east of their location and he did not intend to get involved with them either.

The sails of the other craft were visible for this entire time, so Tim altered course to port again and headed west, hoping to shake the schooner off his stern but the schooner had a larger sail area and a sleeker hull, so it was able to sail faster and soon caught up with them.

There was no option but to allow the schooner to close up on the Triple Tee. At about two hundred yards, Tim took a good look at the schooner with his old telescope and noted that it was in fact the Pembroke that was skippered by Ted Dankworth. The main difference that Tim noticed, was that the triangular topsail was not being used.

Tim carefully scanned the crewman who was on the deck and he could see that he was neither

Dankworth nor the crewman, Finnigan, who they had met back in Port Hedland. There was something familiar about his appearance, but Tim just could not recall where he may have seen him before.

As the Pembroke came closer, the crewman hailed them and called them to heave to, so they could drift alongside in the quiet waters.

It was at this point that Tim recognised the crewman's appearance. When he was skipper on the pearling boat, eighteen years ago, he had a mixture of crew. Chinese, Indian, Indonesian and a few Makassans made up the majority of his crew. Although he didn't recognise the individual, he did recognise the race to which he belongs.

This bloke was a Makassan and from his previous knowledge, the Makassan fishermen or pirates were not a group to get involved with. In fact, he learned that involvement with them usually turned out badly.

Presently a second crewman presented himself on the deck and Tim was, by this time, very suspicious of their intentions. He quietly instructed Bethan to carefully and quietly take the revolvers from their storage place, load and have them ready for him when he calls for them.

Before the Pembroke came alongside, Tim could see that both men were armed with knives of a vicious appearance. He was certain by their manner, that they did wish to cause them harm but he could not know the reason behind their intention.

They called out to him in broken English and said they wish to board his vessel. Tim told them that one of them may come aboard but first he must relinquish his weapon as we don't have weapons like that on board this boat. After some discussion between the men in their own language, the first crewman removed his knife from his belt, aimed and threw it at Tim. The knife caught Tim on the sleeve. It did not mark his skin but stuck into the timber of the cabin, trapping his arm by the sleeve of his shirt. With a swift tug he freed himself and at this time one of the men took hold of a rope which was attached to the mast top and began to swing across the void, intending to land on board the Triple Tee.

As Tim had worked with the Makassan men previously, he could understand some of their language and from what he understood, it was not their intention to leave the weapons behind and he heard the mention of a woman. To Tim's mind that would probably mean they wished to take her hostage or do harm to her.

Tim had Bethan hand him the revolver and he dropped to one knee and with both hands on the pistol grip he aimed at the man on the rope and fired off two shots. The first shot grazed the man's left arm but the second shot was more accurate. It hit the man high in the right side of the chest causing him to release his grip on the rope and he fell into the water, where he made no further movement.

The other crewman immediately aimed and threw his knife at Tim, missing him by barely inches. At this point Tim repeated his procedure and disposed of the second man by taking two shots to complete this mission once again. The second Makassan pirate also fell overboard and ceased moving after several seconds.

He handed the used revolver back to Bethan and had her reload it, just in case there was further use for the weapon.

Tim was shaking like a leaf. He had been involved in the death of Blacksie all those years ago but it wasn't necessarily by his hand. Blacksie had simply tripped over Tim's boot. But this was different. Tim had never intentionally shot and killed a man before and the memory of that action, would haunt him for many years to come. To convince himself of his actions, he kept in mind the recollection of the words of Makassan which he heard from the two men and was satisfying himself that he did what he did for the safety of his family.

During all this time, the two boys had remained in the cabin but were looking out through the portholes and were able to see everything which happened. Before Tim called the others to the deck, he carefully scanned the boat which lay alongside and caught the sight of the slightest movement in the cabin. Tim could not be sure that it wasn't a reflection on the glass of the porthole but it looked like movement to him.

He called out but did not receive any reply, so he fired two shots into the air and could see further movement, just as he had done before. He called out that he was going to board the Pembroke and received no answer at all. With a freshly reloaded revolver tucked into the back of his waistband, he stepped onto the Pembroke after having told the boys to keep a careful eye out for any movement and yell out should they do so. He very carefully crept along the deck until he came to the open hatch of the cabin. Inside he could see Ted Dankworth tied, gagged and bound, lying on the deck of the cabin. He was bleeding from a wound on his side near the waist.

Tim quickly removed the gag and the bindings from his legs and arms while asking what had happened to him. Dankworth told him that they were set upon in a similar manner as just had happened but the other craft was badly damaged and sank soon after the two men came aboard. They knifed his crewman, Finnigan, and threw him overboard and Dankworth didn't even know if Finnigan was dead or not but with that being three days ago, he assumed that by now he would be.

Dankworth assured Tim that no one else was aboard as there were just the two of them, as Tim had seen before back in port.

Tim returned to his own boat and told them what had happened. He had the boys take hourly turns to keep a watch from the masthead for any other vessels which may be in the area. So, with Bethan and the first aid kit, the two of them returned to the Pembroke and carefully attended to Dankworth's injury. Luckily it was only a flesh wound which Bethan was able to apply a couple of stitches to, to bring the flesh together so the healing process could begin. There was no anaesthetic and Pembroke had to bite down on a piece of wood as the needle was used.

Chapter Seventeen

Tim and the boys set only the jib sails of both vessels and one of the boys became helmsman on the Pembroke, as now Tim had to skipper both boats at the same time and it was fraught with difficulties.

Ted was not up to doing any physical work just yet, as he would need a few days to recover from his knife wound. George would stay on the Triple Tee with Bethan and Ted, while Tim and Charles would man the Pembroke.

Although one of the boats was a schooner and the other a ketch. The sail set up was much the same and in a few hours they had it all sorted out so they could set sail, again heading for Babington's Island.

As they sailed along sedately, separated by fifty yards, Tim compared the compass of both boats and found them to be accurate. He plotted his course and with all their delays, they should be approaching the island by nightfall in two days.

Being the good skipper that he was, he had recorded their changes of direction for the last few days and with a good sun shot with the sextant that morning, was satisfied of their position.

There was a five-knot westerly breeze blowing with a three-foot swell, so the sailing was very smooth.

By taking four-hour watches, they were able to keep on station with each other. Bethan had the most to do, she needed to keep an eye on Ted, to make sure he was recovering well and cooking some freshly caught fish for their meals. George did give her some leeway with her watches, as he could see that she was under a fair bit of stress with all that she needed to do each day. But they were able to manage their watches as well as keep abreast of all the duties that were necessary to keep both boats safe.

By the end of the second day, Ted was up and about and able to take the helm for a short period during Bethan's watch, so this allowed Bethan to get some much-needed sleep in her bunk. As the seas were in their favour, Tim had allowed this but Ted was told that should he feel crook or his wound open up, he must rest, as he may be needed in a few days. Bethan was happy with Ted's recovery and was pleased that there appeared to be no infection from the knife wound.

Each of the boys would climb the mast on their boats at the beginning and ends of their watches, to keep an eye out for anything out of the ordinary. Tim was aware that there are exposed rocks near Babington's Island and he wanted to know just as soon as possible should they be approaching, just in case his navigation was out of kilter.

Tim had taken his sextant, charts and map with him when he boarded the Pembroke, just on the off chance that Ted should become inquisitive. And to keep track of their process as the sailed towards their destination.

By Midday on the second day, Charlie was the first to notice a change on the horizon. "Broken water dead ahead!", he yelled out at the top of his voice. This fitted well with Tim's navigation and he was satisfied that they were approaching Babington's Island. Half an hour later he called back to the deck again "Land Ho!" as once again he pointed dead ahead.

He carefully worked around to the north of the island and about half a mile offshore, called for both boats to heave to and drop anchor about fifty yards apart.

When he was sure that the anchors were holding fast, Tim and Charlie left the Pembroke by the dinghy and boarded the Triple Tee.

Now was the time to discuss how they were going to engage with Ted.

It seems that both of their grandfather's served on board the Vertigo under the command of Commander K.J. Babington. Both of them had made some record of their time on board but only Tim's grandfather was left in charge of the map and details of how to find the treasure.

Ted and Tim discussed their situation into the night and just after dark, they agreed that Ted would take a quarter of the treasure and the remaining three quarters would be shared by Tim's family.

This was of course if there was any treasure to find.

The following day Tim and George took the dinghy and rowed to the island and kept a careful eye out for the rocks which were marked on Babington's Treasure Map of Babington's to see if it was navigable. It was a rising tide, so the rowing to the mouth of the tidal creek was an easy task. With a rising tide like this, Tim was satisfied that they could navigate both boats to the creek mouth. Now it was time to follow the creek inland to determine if any features mentioned on Babington's map became evident.

They followed the mangrove lined creek through several bends and then a turn to starboard of about one hundred and seventy degrees.

When they rounded the next bend, there jutting out from the bank, was the remains of a stone jetty. To the left of the stone jetty was a stretch of sand which would make a great beach, even at high tide.

There seemed to be what looked like a structure which had been covered over by the tropical vines. It was large. Maybe this is the remains of the Dutch ship the Merkurius.

As the dinghy was beached, Tim and George, both had a great shock at the same time. There were fresh footprints on the sand, above the high tide mark. Before they could overcome the shock of that revelation they heard a weak voice calling from the undergrowth. They both raced over to where the sound was coming from and found a man laying down with freshly broken branches covering much of his body. Having reached the side of the man, they could see that although he was still alive, he was in bad shape. It was then that Tim recognised the man. It was Finnigan, Ted Dankworth's crewman.

They gave him some water to drink, as he must have been dehydrated and after a few minutes Finnigan seemed to recognise Tim and thanked them for their help with a very hoarse, croaky voice.

He was bundled into the dinghy and against the incoming tide, they rowed back out of the creek and tied up beside the Triple Tee. There was a lot of yelling going on and this roused Ted who was asleep on his bunk in the Pembroke.

Once he was on board, Bethan looked at him and found his knife wound, just as Ted had told them several days ago. Finnigan had packed the wound tightly with his shirt and this had stemmed the flow of blood and saved his life. He was given several of the wheatmeal biscuits to eat and after an hour or so, he was ready to talk for a short time. Before he began talking, George had brought Ted from the Pembroke so he could meet up with his mate again and listen to his story.

Luckily for Finnigan, the knife wound was more of a surprise to him than a bad wound. It was just skin deep but initially bled profusely and Bethan soon had this attended to in her usual professional manner.

Apparently Finnigan had gone over the side, not only from the thrust of the knife wound but also because he was pushed by one of those men who had pirated their boat. He dived under the water and hung around the stern of the boat out of sight, while he attended to the wound. He let go of the boat as it got under way again and some timber from the sunken boat floated by and he was able to grab this and hang on. For two days he hung onto the timber and the running current carried him to the mouth of the creek. He was able to paddle the makeshift timber raft along the creek on the rising tide and made it to the beach. He had been there for two days and was nearly finished when he thought he was dreaming that he heard English speaking voices, so he called out and that is what Tim and Charles had heard.

Chapter Eighteen

The morning after Finnegan was recovered from the beach, Tim set about motoring the Triple Tee through the mouth of the creek and up to a suitable anchorage close to the remains of the old stone jetty. He was able to follow the path which Babington had marked on his map, as it showed the same detail as they had found the day before. They needed to head between the shoreline and the reef. Then a sharp seventy-five degree turn to starboard took them between two exposed rocks. This was followed by a two hundred degree turn to port and then at the mouth of the creek a further turn to port.

The first section of the creek was aptly named on Babington's map, as it was straight as a Gunbarrel. This was followed by that one hundred and seventy degree turn to starboard and they returned to the place near to where they found Finnigan the previous day.

After carefully mooring the Triple Tee, several of them rowed back to the Pembroke on the falling tide and with the next tide, motored it into the creek, carefully following the exact same route and moored close to the Triple Tee.

The creek was deep enough at this point to allow both boats to remain upright at low tide. The keels must have been close to scraping the bottom, which was mostly silt and would not do any damage, except polish off some of the weed which has grown there.

The morning after they had satisfactorily moored the boats, they set about exploring the area to see what may remain of any habitation from a hundred and ten years ago.

They already noted the remains of the stone jetty. What Tim thought may have been the hulk of the Mercurius, may well be correct, because there are remains of oak timber under the vines but it was well rotten and not of any use to them. The old stonework which was described on the map as "The Palace" was still visible but the vines and undergrowth had taken hold and the area was well overgrown. The stonework was still standing and appears solid, so this may be of use to them later, should that become necessary.

The boys rowed the dinghy up the creek as far as they were able to and found the going very heavy, once they beached the dinghy. They would need to clear away much of the vines and undergrowth if they were going to make any headway to the hill which Charlie had spotted from his perch at the top of the aft mast of the Pembroke.

It took them a few days to explore the area before Tim and Ted were satisfied that they were on the island as described by Babington and recorded on his hand drawn map.

Finnigan was recovering well but needed to rest as he was still weak from his ordeal. He would stay on board and be restricted to only light duties and he was willing to comply.

Thinking that it would be good to live away from the boats for a while, they set about clearing up "The Palace". They cut some of the taller mangroves and made a roof to keep the sun out. It probably would not stop any rain unless they were able to stretch a sail over the top, so they would keep that in mind should a rainstorm come their way.

They made their camp within the walls of "The Palace" and brought in bedding and some cooking utensils. The boys scouted around an assembled a good heap of suitable firewood, some of which was dry enough to make a fire. This took them several hours to complete and everyone was beginning to become restless to know if there was any treasure in the location as shown on Babington's map.

Tim was prepared for the prospect of having to cut their way through the jungle undergrowth and brought with them several machetes and axes along with a crowbar to do the job.

The dinghies were rowed to the extreme of the creek and by following the compass, they slowly hacked their way through the dense jungle. It was tough going and the boys seemed to be more energetic than the older men, so they did the brunt of the work. After several hours, Tim called a halt and they all stopped for a well-earned break. They sat on the ground for a few minutes to catch their breath and then back into the work again. By nightfall, they had made over half the distance to the base of the hill.

On returning to the camp in The Palace, they saw that Bethan had a good meal ready for them. It was pretty basic as the dried mutton which they had, was almost completely consumed but they did have enough dried vegetables for another week. That night was their first on land for weeks and they all slept soundly.

Next morning, Finnigan was up with the rest of them and Ted suggested that he could spend some time doing his favourite pastime and catch enough fish to last them for a few days. That which they didn't consume right away could be dried in the sun and kept for a later meal. So, Finnigan spent his morning busy with the fishing line but in the afternoon, he spent some time searching out some of the local vegetation to see if he could find something suitable for their consumption. After tasting a very small amount of several different plants with no side effects, he selected a few samples to take back to the kitchen.

Tim, Ted and the boys, set off once again to complete their way to the hill which is purported to house Bat Cave. They reached the base of the hill by midday and took some time to rest before climbing to where an entrance to a cave might exist. After several hours of searching, they removed some undergrowth and vines to expose an opening which must be the cave.

The floor of the cave was strewn with rocks and boulders but they were able to scramble over or around them and made their way inside the cave. There was sufficient headroom for them all to stand and once around a corner the light began to fade.

Suddenly there was a fluttering of tiny wings and several hundred bats flew past their heads and exited the cave through the mouth. They all dropped to the rocky floor but there was no danger to them from these bats.

As the day was coming to an end, the light in the cave dimmed and they could not see to advance any further. They were satisfied that this was the Bat Cave as described by Babington, so they headed back to the camp and took some time to tell Bethan and Finnigan of their experience. Finnigan showed them his catch and they tasted some of the vegetation which he brought back from his foraging exercise. Tim noticed, at once, a plant which he was conversant with. Samphire was a plant that the station sheep used to graze on and he knew it was safe for them to eat. A bit salty to the taste but when rinsed with some of the fresh water they found in a pool in the cave, it was quite palatable in small amounts but did taste a lot better if it was boiled for a few minutes.

Tim had equipped his trip with a few lanterns as he was prepared for the cave excursion and these turned out to be very useful. Once around the corner, where they had completed their way the day before, they lit the lanterns and continued forward.

Babington's code mentioned something about "under rocks", so they scouted around and found a rock which looks like it didn't quite belong. It was a different colour to the other rocks and they suspected that this may be the rock which covered the boxes of loot that they were searching for. It must have been carried in from the outside when the loot was planted there. Immediately they tried moving the rock but it was far too large and heavy, for even the four of them to shift.

They would need some heavier tools to deal with the large rock that was preventing them from exploring its underside.

In the dinghy, Tim had loaded a crowbar, heavy hammer and bolster that would be helpful in breaking down the large rock. By using the crowbar as a fulcrum, the rock would still not budge, so they tried the hammer and bolster and made a few marks in line across the middle of the rock. If all went well this should break the rock into two pieces and they should be moveable. After several hours of work on the hammer and bolster, and changing operators frequently, a crack appeared across the middle of the rock. With the crowbar inserted and used as a fulcrum, one half of the rock budged a little.

Tim got to thinking that Babington's men would not have been able to move a rock of this nature, so maybe this is not the correct location. Upon further investigation, he could see where part of the roof of the cave had been exposed at a later time than the rest and that perhaps this large rock had fallen from the roof after the treasure had been laid here.

With more effort they were able to move the section of the rock away and could see more smaller rocks beneath. They continued removing both sections of the large rock out of the way and began work on moving one of the rocks which had laid beneath it. These newly exposed rocks were more of a size that Babington's men may have been able to move. A hundred and ten years ago, back in the days of large sailing ships, the men would have been more used to hard physical work and this task may have been so much easier for them. But they kept at the task with the crowbar and any lever that they could find and presently one of the more accessible rocks was moved aside and beneath where it had laid, was the first time they had a look at a wooden box. Tim was careful that they shouldn't break the wooden box, so he suggested that they continue working to remove the other rocks that was hiding the other section of the box.

Once they had the next rock out of the way, they discovered that there were two boxes that had been laid here before the rocks were laid on top of them. Once this second box was discovered, they found that another rock needed to be removed to allow them access to that box.

Before they could get the last rock dislodged and out of the way, the last of the lanterns ran out of fuel and darkness descended upon them, so work had to cease for the day. As their eyes become used to the new low light condition, they could just see to make their way from the cave. Once outside, they found that the sun had already set and the moon was well up into the sky.

Chapter Nineteen

There was just sufficient light to make their way down to the dinghy and row back to The Palace. Bethan had a lantern alight, so they were able to find their way back quite safely. Once they arrived, there was a lot of excitement in the camp, as the four of them all tried to talk at the same time, explaining what they had been able to find out with their expedition today.

While they told what was found, Bethan provided them with a large meal of fresh fish that Finnigan had caught that afternoon. The samphire provided a salty taste to the fish. After all that hard work that each of them had done during the day, sleep overtook them very soon after the meal was completed.

The sunrise was very spectacular in the morning and with a shift in the breeze, Tim was concerned that a change in the weather was imminent. He suggested that they should get a good start on their recovery operation this morning and try to get out of the tidal creek on the next high tide which was due in six hours. If they missed that high tide, the next one would be during the night and Tim didn't think that that was an option. If they left it until the following high tide, there was a chance that this weather change would make it very difficult for them for several days.

Both dinghies were rowed upstream to the end of the creek with freshly refuelled lanterns and a few more tools which may come in handy.

As soon as they returned to the location of their work last night, they continued with the careful removal of the rocks from the second box. It was heavy work, particularly for Ted as he was still recovering from his wound. Every time that he bent over to take hold of something, a pain would shoot across his abdomen, so he was careful to not over do his activity.

With more rocks or boulders that were removed from the boxes, it was evident that there were more boxes stored here. Now it became a race to remove as many rocks as possible to uncover all the boxes. By midday, they took a break and had a lunch of fish which Bethan had provided for them. The short break was just what they needed and they worked hard for another hour and found that they had exposed four boxes. Now was the task to remove the boxes from their hiding place.

Just enough pebbles and soil were removed to allow a rope to pass under the corners of the first box and with the use of the crowbar as a crossbar, three of them were able to remove the box and carefully stand it aside.

They all congregated around the box as they worked out how to unlock it. The lock was very sturdy and Tim suggested that they should carry it down to one of the dinghies, them come back for the other boxes and take them to the dinghies also and work out how to unlock them back at The Palace.

He was very concerned that they should be out of the creek in a few hours and didn't think that any delays would be advised.

Presently two boxes were loaded into each dinghy and rowed back to The Palace by mid-afternoon.

The wind had picked up and the sky was by now completely overcast, with the lower clouds travelling at a fast rate and Tim's leg was causing him a lot of pain, as it usually did with the change of weather.

A storm was imminent.

The tide had just peaked and Tim was becoming very concerned that they only had minutes to clear the creek before the storm hit them.

With so much to do, break camp, load the boxes, tools, their bedding and cooking gear back onto the boats, they had run out of time.

They were not going to be able to leave their mooring now for a few days, if this was the tropical storm that Tim was so concerned about. He reckoned that it would last for three or four days and everything would become very rough. He had the boys retrieve the mainsails from the Triple Tee and once they had returned with these, they set about making The Palace rainproof.

The squally rain began, just as they had the last of the lashings in place. At least they had a dry place to stay on the bank of the creek. Had they been on board the boats, they would have a rough time, so this would be the better accommodation option for the duration of the storm.

At least whilst the storm raged and they were able to keep dry, they had the chance to work out how to unlock the boxes. The old locks had seized up and were no longer able to be operated, so the staple that they were attached to was cut out, allowing for the hasp to be loosened and then carefully the lid of the first box was raised, displaying its contents.

The box which weighed over two hundred pounds was filled to the brim with smaller boxes full of coins. Most of the coins were gold and some others were silver.

Tim was prepared and he had some sketches of some of the old Dutch and VOC coins. He kept these sketches in the chest with the old telescope, sextant and charts. He had brought this ashore when they set up camp in The Palace. He compared the coins with his sketches and found many of them to be very similar to the seventeenth century VOC coins, all with the VOC imprint on them. Many of the others were Dutch Ducats. There were a few other coins in the little boxes, but the VOC coins were the most prevalent.

They proceeded to open the other boxes and they all held the same amount of coins as the first box that they opened.

Everyone was agasp at what they found in the four boxes. They had no idea of the value, except that there was enough money here to keep them and their families comfortable for many years to come. Of course, they would need to have it converted to English pounds for them to be able to spend the money but that was a problem that they would attend to at a later date.

The last box held some old paperwork which had not lasted well in storage. Tim kept these aside with the intention to have it restored and valued once they returned home.

As per the agreement that was struck with Ted, Tim suggested that Ted should select one of the boxes for himself and then he would keep the other three for himself and his family.

Of course, that deal was struck before Finnigan had been rescued. There was no mention of this fact at the time but it was to become a problem in a few days.

Chapter Twenty

The storm was worse than Tim had first predicted. It lasted for three days and with the horizontal rain, water was entering the palace through the rock walls. It was necessary to dig shallow drains inside the walls to drain the water away from their remaining stores and their bedding.

By the last day of the storm, Tim had taken notice that there was a change in Finnigan. He was sullener and more distant than he had been in the days leading up to this point. Because of his injury, he was not able to take part in the recovery of the treasure but he was able to keep his hand in at fishing and gathering some of the samphire that they relied on for their food.

Fresh water was not a problem and while they had the sails over the roof of the palace, they were able to fill all of their water containers and tanks on both boats. The boys did most of this work and returned very wet, after each venture outside. Luckily the weather was tropical warm, so they didn't suffer from the cold had they been in that situation back home.

When Finnigan had taken a walk in the last of the rain to catch a few fish, Tim took Ted aside and spoke about his thoughts about Finnigan. Ted had noticed that change too and was surprised, as Finnigan had always been a happy-go-lucky sort of bloke and nothing much seemed to worry him. It seemed to be so out of character for him.

Upon his return, Ted took Finnigan aside and asked him if there was anything bothering him, apart from the confinement because of the rain. Finnigan had told him that all was good and that he just felt a bit off, telling Ted that it may be a reaction to his ordeal from last week.

They had been on the island for over a week and everyone was getting a bit edgy, wanting to get back to sea and on the way home.

The rain had ceased and the wind had dropped to a stiff breeze, so Tim suggested that they should load everything back onto the boats and make ready to sail on the next tide.

At this point it all turned upside down.

Finnigan took his filleting knife and grabbed Bethan from behind, holding the filleting knife just in front of Bethan's throat. This move took everyone by surprize and despite all of the requests for him to be sensible about his situation, he held his stance and demanded that he would take the Pembroke with three boxes of the treasure and leave her safe.

Tim could see that he was in a no-win situation here and feared for the safety and life of his wife. He loved her and was not about to allow anything to happen to her.

He even considered getting on board the Triple Tee, taking one of the revolvers and disposing of Finnigan, but he dismissed this idea as too dangerous.

He took Ted's glance and they both nodded, indicating that they would agree to his requests.

Tim, Ted and the boys began to move the big boxes down to the water's edge so they could be loaded onto the Pembroke. They had to ferry them out in the dinghy and as they could only take one at a time, the progress was slow. Tim kept an eye on Bethan just to make sure she was faring well enough. She said that she was okay and they should continue with their work.

The Pembroke was loaded and almost ready for sea. Finnigan moved down to the waters' edge and sensing no danger, he released Bethan and taking the dinghy, rowed out to the Pembroke. He called to Ted to join him on his own boat but Ted refused, saying that he would rather stay with Tim and his family. Tim nodded to Ted, suggesting that that was okay with him.

Finnigan started the motor and after weighing the anchor, proceeded to motor downstream on the creek, leaving the dinghy behind.

The tide was flowing out quite quickly and Finnigan had a bit of trouble keeping the boat on course. He grounded once but the flow of the tide freed the boat and he continued on.

Little did he know that there was a particular course which needed to be followed in order to clear the mouth of the creek and avoid the reefs. He was unwell and below deck when they entered the mouth and had no idea of the path which they had taken. He realised that there were a few rocky outcrops near the mouth when he reached them. The reef that he could not see was quite shallow and the boat foundered on the submerged reef causing the boat to list to port rather quickly. This motion threw Finnigan against the spar, knocking him unconscious. The boat continued to be battered by the outgoing tide and was raised up when the swell met the outgoing tide.

The boat crashed into the reef and become stuck with the outgoing tide pushing it outwards while the swell was pushing it in the other direction each time that it rolled in. After half an hour of this battering, the schooner began breaking apart, being only partly submerged.

There was no sign of Finnigan.

They all watched this event happening as they had rowed the dinghies downstream following the Pembroke. They could see where it had ended up on the reef and offered Ted their commiserations for the loss of his boat. Bethan was in one of the dinghies and although was badly shaken, she was not injured.

Now that they had done all that hard work in recovering the boxes from the cave and only retaining one of the four boxes for themselves, they were all very disappointed, not so much for Finnigan but for the loss of all of those coins.

The boys immediately came up with the idea that just as soon as the weather abated and on the slack tide, they should dive down on the wreck and see if they could locate the boxes which Finnigan had loaded on board.

Tim was sceptical but knew that the idea had good merit.

They waited near the wreck site for an hour for the tide to slacken and by this time the swell had reduced sufficiently for one of them to dive down and check to see if he could locate the boxes.

On his first dive, Charles found one and it was still intact. Upon surfacing he called for a rope so that he could tie it to the box and those in the dinghy could begin to haul it up. The box was heavy so he fitted another rope to the box and attached the other end to all of the life vests tied together. By shortening this rope some of the weight of the box was reduced and allowed the others to recover it. Another box, also still intact was found when George made his dive. He followed the same procedure as Charles had and shortly that box was also hauled aboard the dinghy. With two boxes on the dinghy the gunnels were just above the water line , so it was taken back to the Triple Tee where the boxes were transferred. When the dinghy returned, Charles had located the third box and had a rope ready for those on the dinghy to haul it in.

The last box was a bit more difficult to find, as it was lodged under some of the boats broken timbers jammed into the reef. Using a saw and brute strength, the boys soon had it free and just as the tide began it inwards flow, they hauled the last box onto the dinghy.

By this time, it was just on dark, so they returned to the Triple Tee and stowed the last of the boxes on board.

It was too late to make the run downstream and with the tide running the wrong way for them, they remained at their mooring until next morning.

The following morning was bright sunshine with just a gentle southerly blowing. The tide was nearing its peak as they left their moorings and motored downstream. By following the course that they had taken to enter the creek mouth, they successfully made it out into the open sea.

They dropped Ted off in Port Hedland so he could make his own way home with his one box and after spending some time with Bert and his family they sailed off to the west, homeward bound.

The end.

The Author

David Kentish spent his early years on the family dairy farm just south of Perth in Western Australia near the small settlement of Keysbrook.

Before the time of broadcast television, his father, J. Lance Kentish, spent time in the evenings inventing and telling stories about the bush animals, the talking red-gum tree and the magic carpet to his family.

David has continued in a similar vein with the telling of stories set in the Australian bush and outback.

He and his wife Barbara enjoy travelling with their car and caravan in and around the Australian outback and bush. This is where he gets most of his inspiration which has led to a collection of stories that marvel at the many locations which they have visited and the characters whom they have met.

Here are some of what he has already completed:

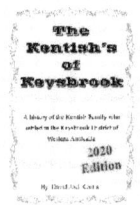

Paperback and E-book	Paperback and E-book	Paperback and E-book	Paperback and E-book

Paperback and E-book	Paperback and E-book	Paperback and E-book	Paperback and E-book

https://david-kentish.square.site

Scan the QR code for more stories to enjoy.

Happy reading and enjoy everything that you do.

David Kentish

www.ingramcontent.com/pod-product-compliance
Lightning Source LLC
Chambersburg PA
CBHW051836020726
47502CB00005B/1807